THE LONG RUN

RUTH PRICE

& SARAH CARMICHAEL

TABLE OF CONTENTS

ACKNOWLEDGMENTS

Grace and praises first go to the Almighty God who has given me this wonderful opportunity to share my stories with the world! Next, I have to thank my family who has been my rock not only in my artistic endeavors but also through the myriad of health issues I've had recently.

I also thank Ruth and the ladies of Global Grafx Press's Family Christian Bookstore for allowing me work with you for self-publishing. And lastly, I thank you for reading this book. There are lots of books you could be reading now, and you've chosen mine. Thank you and God Bless!

CHAPTER ONE

Rod Travis was contemplating going home, though the shady spot he had taken under a tree was making it difficult not to simply fall into a doze, when a movement in the corner of his peripheral vision made him turn his head instinctively. He caught sight of the source of the movement: a young boy dressed plainly in old-fashioned clothing, at most fourteen or fifteen years old with a straw hat on his head, was darting off from the direction of one of the buildings. Almost at once, Rod's passing curiosity developed into intense interest. He had always had an eye for running technique—and that eye, that ability to train young athletes into fine-tuned machines had gotten him his job and more than a few accolades as a coach for Lancaster County.

The boy's simple clothes did nothing to blur the eye-pleasing way he moved, and Rod felt a spurt of professional excitement, watching the boy. He moved with clean—if untrained—precision, carrying himself lightly on feet that seemed to know the terrain underneath perfectly. The boy's elbows were tight to his sides, and his head was perfectly straight on his neck; not tilted down or up. *Put a uniform on him and he'd be right in place with some of the Juniors or Seniors,* Rod thought, comparing the boy's movements to the more practiced members of the high school team he oversaw. Of course, the kid wasn't likely to be in the high school at all— he looked too young—but it was never too early to recruit for the team. Someone so promising at such a young age would be easy to mold into the kind of young athlete that won plenty of track meets—maybe even cross-country as well, Rod thought, seeing the way the boy paced himself. It would be easy, and a joy, to train someone who already had so many of the raw ingredients that made a runner excel.

Rod watched the boy for a moment longer, trying to figure out where he was going to; he wanted to talk to him—the impulse to recruit a new runner to the team, even if it was early days, was strong. He saw the boy turn onto a rough-hewn road and looked around. His Jeep was only a couple of yards away, where he'd left it, tempted by the warm sunshine and pretty landscape of the area to take a little break on his errands.

He fumbled for the keys in his pocket as he stood quickly, hurrying over to the Jeep. He didn't want to scare the boy; but he knew that whoever the child was, he would make a great addition to any team. He glanced in the direction that the boy had gone and caught sight of him again, shaking his head with a little smile on his face. The kid would be great—and Rod started planning to groom the kid for college, even. Or, Rod thought, admiring the pacing and form of the runner just a moment longer as he unlocked the door to the car and opened it, he might even persuade the boy to try for the Olympics.

Rod started up the Jeep and turned onto the road, continuing to watch the boy. Most of his current team would have been at least a little fatigued—but the boy showed the stamina of a Masaai warrior.

Rod shook his head, smiling to himself once more. It was sheer luck, and he blessed the providence that had brought him to rest under that particular tree, where he'd catch sight of such a promising young runner. He decided not to waste any more time in admiring the boy and pulled onto the road, following the direction the child was traveling. He didn't want to frighten him; as he approached it was clear that the boy was barely aware of the world around him, a beatific smile on his face, sheer joy of movement in his eyes.

Rod slowed as he came abreast of the lad—and thought that he might be as young as thirteen, up close. "Hey, kid!" Rod said, stopping the Jeep. The boy turned his head, his eyes widening in brief confusion and wonder at the sight of him leaning out through the Jeep's window.

"Me?" The boy asked, his brows coming together in a frown of confusion. Rod nodded, and the boy stopped, cheeks flushed and a little sweat on his brow, but not looking nearly as fatigued as some of the runners Rod had on his team, even after running a fair distance at such a pace. "May I help you?" The boy's words were accented, and Rod thought that the kid was having a little trouble—maybe remembering the correct words.

"What's your name?" Rod asked. "I'm coach Rod." The boy hesitated for just a moment, considering the question.

"I am called David, sir. David Beiler." Again that slight accent—Rod tried to remember, tried to place it, along with the formality that went with it. He decided to think about it later.

"Son, you're a great runner," Rod said, nodding firmly with a smile. "It's obvious to see you take great joy in it—as you should, it's a gift." The boy's color deepened and he glanced at the ground for a moment. "I'm the coach over at the high school, track and field, cross-country. I know you're probably a bit young for it, but do you think you'd consider joining the team?"

The boy's reaction startled and confused Rod, who was expecting amazement—maybe pleasure. Instead the flush left the boy's face as it paled, and David's eyes widened in something that was less pleased amazement and more utter confusion.

"Nee! I can't!" The boy stared at him for a moment longer, shaking his head, and Rod was about to ask him what was wrong, why he was so startled; but the next moment, the boy

took off once more, moving at an even more amazing pace—
so quickly that Rod was stunned.

He watched as the boy darted down the road, head bent
forward, using the same excellent raw form he had seen before
but moving so much faster that it was incredible to see. Rod
stared after the boy in mute respect for such natural talent.

He shook himself out of his shock and watched the boy
heading towards a complex of low, plain buildings; it was
obvious that he was heading for one in particular, and Rod
decided to follow him—it made sense to him that the boy was
likely heading home, and it would be easier, he hoped, to talk
to the boy's parents than to the boy himself. *Probably shy, like
a lot of the country folks out here,* Rod thought to himself.
*Godly, not the kind to put himself forward. I probably startled
the daylights out of him.*

He realized vaguely that the boy was one of the Amish—
but that shouldn't make any difference, he thought. The boy
was naturally talented; and Rod had a vague idea that the
Amish sent their kids to school anyway. He'd make sure that
he explained to the parents that there would be no interference
in the child's schoolwork—in fact, in order to be on the team,
he would have to maintain good grades—and there would be
no issues with any religious observances that the family had.

Rod followed the boy at a safe distance, not wanting to
startle him again; the roads were rough, suited to buggies and
walking, but not so well made that a startled person wouldn't

stand a risk of taking a tumble. He watched as David rushed forward, heading for a small home among the complex, and sped forward in the Jeep, determined to get in another chance to talk to someone about the child's impressive talent.

Rod pulled the Jeep to, and leaped out of the car, as he saw the door to the house open, the boy rushing in with barely a word to an older woman who met him; she wore a plain bonnet and simple dress with an apron over it, and looked to be in her middle years—her face lined a little by sun and wind and plain living, but still kindly and gentle. Rod closed the door to the Jeep hard, hurrying as the woman turned to ask the departing boy a question. "Ma'am! Are you that boy's mother?" Rod called out, thinking of nothing but the need to talk to someone—anyone—about David's talent, and his promise as an athlete.

The woman looked up, startled. "May I help you?" she asked him, a look of confusion in her soft eyes. Rod took a deep breath, wishing that David hadn't left so quickly. The interior of the home was dimly lit, but from what Rod could see from the front porch he stepped onto, the whole home was cozy, well made, and clean, if plain.

"Yes," Rod said, focusing on the woman in front of him. "If you're David's mother, I would love to speak to you about your son." The woman looked at him sharply, her lips pressing together in a forbidding way. Rod held his hands up. "Just— just for a moment. I know you're probably a very busy woman, and I am probably… I mean no harm."

"Has my son done you wrong?" the woman asked with concern in her voice.

"No, Ma'am. In fact, I wanted to extend him an opportunity. I saw him running along the road, and he's a natural. I'm coach over at the local high school for track and field, and cross-country; running." Rod realized that the woman's frown was not entirely concern; like the boy, she seemed to be trying to understand what he was saying, as though her knowledge of and comfort with English was less than perfect.

"If his running has disturbed you, I will have him apologize," the woman said cautiously.

"No, Mrs. Beiler—it is Mrs. Beiler, is it not?" The woman hesitated briefly before nodding. "His running didn't bother me at all. In fact, his running is excellent. I hoped I could talk to you about the possibility of him joining the high school track team in a year or so." The woman's reaction to the offer was a mirror of what the boy's had been: she went pale, her eyes widening, and shook her head quickly.

"Nee! He will not join any sports teams, or any schools! At all! Please—leave at once. Right now." It was not quite brusque—it was somehow still polite—but Rod saw as the woman hurriedly moved back into the house, closing the door behind her with a finality that was unmistakable. He sighed, looking at the floor. Slowly, his own behavior—and its inappropriateness to the setting—dawned on him. He shook his head and went back towards the Jeep, trying to think of what he could do to improve the situation. *First of all, it probably wouldn't help to linger on her doorstep. See if you can find another opportunity to talk to them—now obviously isn't a good time.* Rod thought it was a shame; he couldn't understand what would make it a problem for the boy to enjoy a little friendly competition, some development in his ability. He would have to read up, study the Amish culture a little more, and decide on the best course of action to get the child and his parents to understand what the possibilities were.

CHAPTER TWO

Barbara stood by the door for a moment, shock rolling over her in waves. It had been so long since she had spoken to an Englischer that the formalities of it—the strange clipped words and the accent that bent in strange directions—nearly threw her into confusion. To hear that the Englischer wanted her boy— her David—to join a team threw her into a panic. She hoped that she had not been unduly rude to the man, and prayed silently for forgiveness if her shock had led her to something like haughtiness.

She sat down heavily, thinking of the last time she had spoken to Englischers. The visit from the sports coach—and the offer he had made—brought back all the pain of her sister's departure from the community, seeking the company of the Englisch instead of her own kind. Barbara's eyes stung, and she trembled, feeling all the pain of the loss anew; she had put it behind her, or so she had thought. She had trusted to God that her sister had done the right thing, taken the path that made the most sense for her, but to know that Anne was out there, living amongst people who were not her kin, not her community, gave Barbara so much fear that it was hard for her to go a day without thinking of it.

Barbara felt the tears rolling down her cheeks and quickly snatched at the towel draped over her shoulder, burying her face in it as the pain washed through her. She missed Anne; she missed her sister's smiles, the warmth of her eyes, the kindness of her heart. She missed the gentle way that Anne would tease her, the ready laugh when they were alone, joking about a mishap, telling tales between sisters. Losing Anne so soon after her baptism had been like cutting off her own arm, and Barbara had scarcely known how to stop the bleeding feeling she had for her sister's loss. It was as if Anne had died suddenly. When Barbara had been delivered of a girl, the temptation had risen to name her daughter for the sister she had lost—but the Ordnung would forbid it. She had deliberately chosen the name Salome to avoid any thought of the sister who had left the community—either in her own mind or in the minds of others.

Barbara cried until the tears eventually stopped coming, remembering little things about the sister she missed so much; the way that Anne would help her every day, the patience her sister had always had for her incessant questions when they were young together. She had always known her lessons so much faster than Barbara had; when Anne had made the choice to leave, it had shocked everyone. Everyone had always assumed that having made up her mind to be baptized, Anne had gotten every bit of wildness out of herself that a Rumspringa allowed. But there had been, Barbara knew, other temptations—and she couldn't quite condemn her sister, even though she had left on such poor terms.

Finally, Barbara wiped at her face, knowing that it was nearly time for her husband to come home. She would need to make sure that dinner was prepared, that everything was as it should be. She could not let the disturbance affect her dedication to her work. She would discuss it with her husband, and they would talk to their son, after dinner and study. It was important to make sure that they understood each other. But the prospect of losing her son—whose Rumspringa would come in a few short years—weighed on her mind, even as Barbara diligently went about the rest of her tasks for the day. It was a question that every mother faced, she knew. It was one that she should trust to God to provide an answer for. But she had already lost so much—she said a quick prayer in her mind. God would see to it that David came to a good decision. There was nothing more to think about.

CHAPTER THREE

David had been startled—and more than startled soon after—
when the Englischer teacher stopped him; he had been on the
way home with purchases his father had asked him to make for
his carpentry business. Daed was beginning to show him the
way with carpentry, and David was deeply interested in
following his father's business, learning the ways of wood and
how to build things that would last. Daed had told him on more
than one occasion that the same skills that allowed a person to
make a cabinet or a trunk were practical for building a house
as well—though building a house or a barn took many more
men than building smaller items.

As David ran the rest of the way home from his encounter
with the Englischer man, he had to laugh at the thought of
joining an Englisch high school, becoming part of a
competitive team. He had been shocked and dismayed at first;
he had thought that all of the Englisch knew that Amish boys

and girls ended formal schooling strictly after the eighth grade, entering into either farming or apprenticeships with family. He was starting to learn the skills that it would take to be a self-sufficient member of the community, but once he left schooling, then his real education would start.

For now, his father had him working on finishing projects—a few years ago, David had only been allowed to do the very safest, easiest of tasks, such as staining or hammering, but as he came closer to being a grown man, Daed trusted him to learn more—and David was eager to learn.

It was not simple interest in self-sufficiency that made David eager; as he ran, he thought of Salome Lapp, and smiled to himself. He had started to notice her among the other girls their age a couple of years before; her long, blonde hair and deep brown eyes somehow appeared to him—one day, suddenly—to be the most beautiful ornaments that any girl could ever possess. Salome had always been godly and good, with a happy demeanor and a helpful nature—but as David began to notice girls as more than just companions during school, he noticed her more and more. He was anxious to finish his schooling and come of an age where he could appropriately court her—and with that courting, he had every intention of marrying her and remaining within the community.

The idea of giving up that future for something like running made David laugh so much that he was out of breath—a rarity for him—by the time he reached his home. His mother had wanted to know what was so funny; when David had seen the Englischer bring his car to a stop outside of the house, David knew that Mamm would find out soon enough; though a little tingle told him that she would not find it as funny as he did.

Nothing was said about the Englisch man or what he had asked David during dinner; it was a time of quiet family togetherness, and issues like that one were reserved for private conversation. David's brothers and sisters had no need to know about what the Englischer man had said, though there was no secrecy in the family. David knew that he had done the right thing in telling the man "no" definitively, and he knew that his Mamm had done the same. He wondered what she had thought of it—a stranger, an outsider, praising him for something as simple as running.

After dinner, David and his siblings sat in the living room with their parents, and their Daed selected the passage from the bible that they would study that evening. The passage was 1 Samuel 17, and as his Daed read through it, David followed along, thinking carefully of the events. He knew that it was forbidden to try and "interpret" the bible—it was a direct translation of the word of God, not to be cluttered with haughty thoughts about what other meanings there might be, but in his mind he pictured the events, pictured the preparations of the Israelites to battle against the Philistines. David thought that it was strange to think of men of God using violence of any kind—either to defend themselves or to regain their promised lands—but it was not for him to try and understand that difference. There were worldly ways in the bible that the Amish had shunned, ways that were not included in the Ordnung.

After the bible reading for the evening, David returned to his room to pray and think about his day in solitude. There was a great deal to think about: his interactions with his school mates, the work that he was doing with his Daed, and finally the meeting of the Englischer coach.

At first, David thought that it was simply funny; he had no idea that any Englischers had failed to know about the customs of the Amish. Every Englisch person he had ever met had instantly recognized his attire for what it was, and had known that he was Amish, and therefore knew plenty about his culture—a surprising amount in fact. He had been asked sometimes very rude questions.

Once, when he had run into town to make some purchases his father had asked of him, an Englischer woman had told him that it was shameful that his parents cared so little for him that they wouldn't let him have nice clothes or toys, that they made him work from a young age. David had been bemused; it didn't make any sense for him that children should have anything particularly worldly in the way of toys, or that they should be excused from household chores and the needs of the community.

But as he continued to think about the interaction with the Englischer man, David's thoughts began to turn over in his mind. He had never considered competition to be something he could do—he had never really thought about it at all. Even sports amongst the people of his community were about cooperation and fun, not about seeing who was the best at a particular task, or highlighting anyone in the group.

It was a matter of fitness, of getting rid of excess energy in a productive way. David had always had that viewpoint, and though sometimes he was wanted on softball teams because of his ability to run, he had always managed not to put himself forward, not to think about being better at that than his other friends. It was not a talent—it was a simple thing that God had given him, not to be used for prideful purposes but for useful ones.

But as he thought about what the Englischer had said, David wondered what it would be like: to continue on in school beyond the end of primary years, into his adulthood. To become better at running, to compete against other runners. There was no one among his friends who could run as well as David could—no pride was required to know that. It was a simple statement of fact. The few times he had dared to comment on it, his Mamm or Daed had pointed out that being particularly good at something did not mean that it was useful or practical; he should turn his thoughts not onto being a better runner for the sake of being the best, but for the purposes of making his ability useful.

But then, David thought—it would be very different indeed to compete. He had never been in competition before.

It might be fun; to see different runners, to see others who were as good as he was, to see if he was able to keep up with them— or even surpass them. David had seen a race before; the clothing, he knew, would be at an issue, right away. It was far too worldly, too covered in details that a simple-living Amish boy had no need of. But if he could be allowed to run in his own clothing, that might be something.

David smiled to himself, picturing the possibility of assembling with the other runners—he in his normal clothes, they in their uniforms—and setting up to compete. It would, he knew, be a thrill; one of the older boys had taken part in an eating contest of some kind during his Rumspringa, and had quietly told the younger boys about it, shaking his head against the worldly temptation. The older boy had said that he had immediately known that the thrill he felt at winning, the feeling of holding the trophy—a glittery thing of metal and plastic and stone—was wrong, was a temptation.

And so as David reflected on his feelings towards competing with other boys, he realized that he, too, was facing a temptation. He was nearing the time of his own Rumspringa, and he wanted to use it profitably. David had little doubt that he would return to the community at the end of it; he could not imagine a future without marrying, without the steady, loving presence of his family and kin around him, the knowledge that the community as a whole would help any calamity he might meet. The little he knew of the outside world had taught him that it was one of a great deal of coldness; every person was made to fend for themselves, with little reliance on even their family—much less the extended family of the church.

He turned his thoughts instead to Salome Lapp. David smiled to himself with deeper appreciation. They both would be coming to their time of Rumspringa soon—and David knew that it would be the perfect time to think of beginning to court her. He had not said anything of his interest in the girl to his parents, which was right. It gave him a tingle to imagine the possibility of meeting with Salome outside of the frolics and sings that were a central part of life as an Amish youth. David thought—though he could not be sure—that Salome felt the same way towards him. They did not have an opportunity to speak alone, but sometimes when they were in a group together, David could see a little sparkle in her deep brown eyes that made him think that she was thinking of him, just as he considered her.

Because she was still young, Salome's blonde hair was not as confined as it would be when she was an adult, living in the community as a woman looking to wed or married. David thought to himself that it would be a beautiful thing indeed to see her hair tumbled down, out of its usual twist hidden underneath her bonnet, cascading around her shoulders and down her back. He wished that there could be a way to see it without having to wait—but he chastened himself. Impatience, haste, was a sin, just as surely as pride was. He would pray to God to make the right choices that would put him in the path of becoming Salome's husband. He would use his Rumspringa appropriately and make his decision with open eyes, and then they could be together.

David's thoughts wandered along this vein, and he imagined himself as a self-sufficient man of the community, living the way that his Daed did, with a good and godly wife— Salome—to love and to have as his helpmeet. The prospect was sweet, and the temptation of competition, of singling himself out amongst the many and indulging vanity, began to fade in the face of what tradition and education had taught him was the best possible future.

David began to think of the last time that he had seen her. It had been at a frolic; David smiled to himself remembering it. One of the other families in the community had held a barn raising to replace a barn that had burned down in an accident, and David had of course been there with his father several times before to work with the family on carpentry details. When he arrived in the morning, Salome and her mother Sarah had already arrived, ready to do their part in preparing food and drink to serve the men at work. David remembered that Salome's bonnet was just slightly askew on her head—giving him a brief vision of her glorious hair in more detail than he had ever seen. She had gone into the house with her mother only a moment afterward, but the sight of her never left David's mind even as he hammered and helped, listening sharply for his father's call in particular.

As the day progressed, more and more delicious smells came out of the house, and David found himself thinking of

Salome, hard at work inside, following her mother's instructions. He saw her in his mind doing the things he had seen his mother doing so many times: mixing dough, going to retrieve more wood for the stove, kneading bread, going to work on the chickens. David's mental image was so detailed in fact that at one point he forgot to listen for his father, "Black" David's call—and was briefly reprimanded for his distraction. He had been imagining Salome working the bread, her head bent sweetly forward over the board, her hands busy and industrious, a little smear of loose flour streaked across her flushed cheek. It was an image sweet enough to make him forget everything that he was doing—to forget that the world even existed.

By noon, the smells of food being carried out of the big house and onto the tables set up outside were too much to bear for anyone, and David spotted Salome delivering one of the last items quickly, her eyes downcast slightly, her cheeks pink with embarrassment at her tardiness. He had wanted to talk to her then—but he couldn't. Instead he thought about her while he and the other men and boys sat down to the feast, laughing and discussing the barn to be built, the weather, the prospects for the season. When the men were finished, David kept a sharp look on the house and spotted Salome coming out to help the other girls clear. Their gazes met for just a moment, and David felt himself smiling without entirely knowing why—just at the sight of her, the reassuring realization that she was there.

They had gone back to work and David had thought to himself that when the time came for him to court and then to wed, he would do what he could to take a moment—though he knew it was frowned upon—to check in on his wife, to have just one little bit of privacy with her. Some of the other men in the community did this, even though it was not exactly proper—but they loved their wives, and it was said that small improprieties like these were not as important as a loving marriage.

By midafternoon, David was anxious for the break; the barn was nearly completed, and if they managed to finish it before the sun went down, there would be some little time to socialize all together—there would be a few moments where they could spend time as a group, letting the adults talk to each other, while the younger children who could not help were playing. A frolic always made everyone sleep better, especially the children who had so much energy. David drank his water and looked for Salome—she would be among the girls moving around discreetly to clear the table of the various snacks and drinks, he knew it. David thought that of all of the girls he had ever met, he had never known one who was as simply gentle and gracious as Salome. She was always ready to help—eager, even. Her mother brought them as much into the community as possible, after they had finished mourning Salome's father. David had heard Sarah say that they needed to feel as though they were still part of life, however they could manage it—and that because her husband had passed away, and could not participate and give his strength among the men, it fell to her and Salome especially to take up the burden as well as they could, to do more than was required of them with happy hearts.

David's silent prayers were answered; the barn was finished with an hour before the sun would go down, and he and the other boys of his age group milled around, talking, as the girls of their group came out, having finished the work of clearing up. All of the children of the community were eager to be away from their parents—not out of disrespect, but because they had been thinking about their peers, so close to them, but unable to socialize, all day. David had had the benefit of a group of boys and girls around him to venture a few quiet words to the girl who meant so much to him; nothing more meaningful than a question about how her mother was doing, or whether she had started to understand one of their lessons in school better. But he had felt his cheeks warming, and saw that Salome's cheeks became pinker than any effort or heat could have made them, even with just those few brief words spoken between them.

David hoped that there would be a similar opportunity the following Sunday; there was church on that day, and after services were over there would be a sing. Some of the other, older children in their age group were starting to form decided preferences—and David knew that the parents who hosted the sings in their homes were starting to be aware, without saying anything, that courting was on the horizon. For the moment he had to keep his preference for Salome completely to himself, as much as he possibly could. They were both too young to even consider courting. But he hoped—and silently, sitting in his room, David prayed—that there would be the possibility of just a few words between them, something he could think about for the whole week, to store up in his mind in those hours when he was almost idle—though he was never completely idle except when he was asleep. Just the thought of Salome's hair—the way it gleamed ever so slightly in the sun, the sight of it when her bonnet was askew—was enough to send a warm rush through David's body, to make his skin tingle. He wanted to feel that again.

CHAPTER FOUR

Black David—named for his ink-dark hair and brown eyes—
hefted his tools in the sack he carried them in as he approached
the house, carefully stomping on the mat his wife's hands had
made so thoughtfully before he came in through the front door.
It had been a long day of work, but the fatigue in his body—
the slight soreness in his arms and legs, the distant ache in his
back—was welcome. He had long before learned that nothing
ensured a restful sleep like good, hard work—a lesson his own
Daed had taught him, and one that he was imparting to his
kinner. He took a deep breath, smelling the scents of the
promising meal that would be on the table as soon as he arrived
in that room. His wife seemed to always know not only what
would satisfy his hunger best, but also how to make it in such
a way that it was affordable.

As he came into the house, and went into the kitchen to
seek his wife, he saw that while Barbara was as industrious as

ever—the last of the dishes being ferried out by their daughter—there was something amiss about the woman he loved. Her eyes were reddened, her cheeks were pale with vivid spots of color at the top; a sure sign that she had been crying a great deal. But Black David knew that the conversation as to what troubled her was one for a private time. It was not one to have over dinner, or even before dinner. Such sadness was not something like burning a loaf of bread, or a problem with a broken broom. It was something deeper—something that touched his wife's very heart.

And so instead of asking her what was wrong, Black David gave his wife a brief kiss on his way to wash up and put away his tools. If he gave her shoulder a gentle squeeze, if he looked into her sweet, gentle, troubled eyes for a long moment—that was between them, and it was proper. Barbara smiled, brightening at the sight of him, and he saw her nod, just slightly—acknowledging silently that they would talk later.

They all sat down to the table, and Black David noticed with pleasure that the meal was a particularly good one: Sauerbraten with fluffy, rich potato dumplings and red cabbage, biscuits, some ham gravy for the biscuits, some of the leftover relishes of the previous harvest—to clear the pantry for the next harvest, Black David was sure—with jellies and preserves, and the remains of a pie Barbara had baked the previous day, sweet and thick with molasses. Black David helped himself liberally, filling his plate; he was starving after a long day's work, and the meal was one of his very favorites.

After him, his son David served himself, then Barbara, and then their daughter. They paused for a moment, each of them saying their prayers silently, and Black David thanked God for his family, for their good health and wellness, for the solace of hard work, and the closeness he shared with his wife. He thought, finishing his prayers, that he was blessed indeed—that God had given him exactly what suited him best in life, with the warmth of family love, and compatibility with his wife.

As he ate, listening to his children detailing their days at school quietly, David looked at his wife often; he had loved her before he had ever started courting her, and when he had reached the age to find a wife, there had been no question in his mind. God had given him a clear view of his future, and the best way to preserve his happiness. Barbara; her sweetness, her gentleness, her kindness to others, was full of reasons to love.

David had met several Englischer men, had spoken with them from time to time, slightly curious about their lives. During his Rumspringa, he had taken the opportunity to learn as much as he could about what life was like outside of the community, and had never thought anything was missing from his own life when he made the decision to be Baptized. So many men, consumed with their need to have the "best" wife, compared and contrasted, competed and pushed themselves forward in ways that shocked Black David. It was not for him to find the wife who would be the most beautiful, or the wife who would be the most skilled cook or the best keeper of house. He wanted—simply—the wife who would suit him the most, and he had found that in Barbara.

Black David reflected silently that there was something deeply amiss in men who would look at only the physical beauty of the woman they wished to marry; there was so much of deep, spiritual beauty in his wife—so much of the thing called Grace, the ability to love unreservedly, to give herself to others—that even if she had been homely, Black David thought that he would have loved her without thought to any other person. There was something so soul satisfying about the sweet way she smiled at him in the mornings before they went about their separate days; about the way that she greeted him when he returned home, her eyes full of love. It was impossible not to quarrel—two people living in the same home could not avoid it—but they had managed to maintain the peace in their lives and in each other, by knowing when to decide to stop, when to relent, and when to compromise. There was never a word that Black David spoke to his wife only for the purpose of hurting her; the idea of her in pain was too much to want to ever be the cause. There was never a word that Barbara had spoken to him expressly to hurt him. When they had argued, it was always over something specific—and always keeping that specific topic in mind.

An Englisch man, looking to purchase a large set of cabinets from Black David, had once asked him if his life was not very boring; the question had completely confused him. The need for constant excitement was one that he simply could not understand—life itself created more than enough troubles to live through, more than enough of what the Englischers called drama. It was restful, it was comfortable, to not go looking for more stimulation than he had. At any moment, it was possible that he could be injured—or that tragedy could befall his family. It was not something that worried Black David, as much as it was something that he recognized as a fact of living. One could not avoid chance entirely. Some of the men who had been on Rumspringa with him, Black David knew, had done things like going skydiving, or breaking minor laws, for excitement. He had indulged in a few misdemeanors, but nothing that would excite the attention of the Englischer government.

After dinner, there had been the nightly bible study, and Black David had read carefully, focusing on the words of God, thinking about the lesson that the reading imparted. His son was reaching that age—he was nearing the completion of his school years, and would soon be in that restless stage where boys start to become men. Black David had started to increase his son's responsibilities at the shop, but he knew that soon not even the responsibilities of a fully-grown man would be enough to occupy David's mind. Soon his son's thoughts would turn to finding a wife, if they had not already. It would be a difficult time to get the young man through, and though Black David was prepared for some minor inappropriate actions on the part of his son, in weak moments he worried—even with the Bible's eloquent passages on why no man should ever worry but should instead trust in the Lord.

Finally, after the kinner went to their rooms for quiet, private time, Black David was able to see his wife alone. When Barbara went into their bedroom, she sank down onto the bed with a heaviness that Black David could not possibly mistake—she was full of the weight of grief, and he thought to himself of his wife's sister; of his sister-in-law who had left the community after taking her oath. That was one of the only things, he knew, that could bring his wife this low: the memory of that loss.

"What has happened to make you so sad, Barbara?" Black David asked, sitting down next to the woman he loved. He draped one arm lightly around her shoulders, pulling her in close to him. Barbara began to shake, to tremble , and he heard her breath hitching in her throat, heard the valiant attempt to control herself and then she began to cry. He held her for a moment, knowing the pain that she felt was too strong for her to talk, soothing her with gentle rubbing touches along her arm, pulling her in closer. Barbara brought her apron up to her face to wipe away the tears streaming from her eyes as she began to quiet once more.

"I am sorry," Barbara said, taking a deep breath and exhaling it slowly. She looked at him and in spite of the sadness and trouble that was still on his wife's face, Black David was filled with love—she was a beautiful woman, with a gentle smile and kindness in her eyes, and Black David thought that no person who knew her could fail to love her. He pressed a kiss to her forehead.

"You have nothing to be sorry about," Black David said, giving his wife a slight smile. "I could see when I came in that you were troubled by grief; and you still had dinner ready, you still were able to remain composed. I love you dearly, my wife." Barbara mirrored his smile, though her eyes were still watery with tears. "What happened to bring the grief upon you again?" Barbara took another deep breath.

"David came home this afternoon, just fine—but he had apparently attracted the attention of an Englischer teacher of some kind." Barbara explained about how their son had run into the house, how the Englisch man had approached her on the patio, hurriedly telling her about the high school and talking about their son. Black David frowned.

"Did David interrupt the man or something like that?" He asked. Barbara shook her head.

"He saw our son running; the Englischer is some kind of coach, I think—he works with the running team at the high school." Black David nodded slowly. He remembered well that their son's ability had not gone unremarked, even in the community; while it was and could be impressive when used to productive ends, it had often also forced others—including Black David himself—to remark that haste was often wasteful, and that while there was nothing bad about being efficient in one's daily duties, it shouldn't be an excuse for getting them done so quickly that they were not done thoroughly.

Barbara explained that she had made the Englischer man leave. "I am afraid—a little—that he might have found me rude, that he might have thought I was being proud." She frowned. "I hope that I was not acting in a prideful way. But I had to tell him to go away, I had to make him leave." Black David gave her shoulder an approving pat.

"You did just as you should. Nee, our son will not be joining a running team." Barbara nodded her agreement. Black David considered the odd, unexpected visit. It was difficult to not feel a slight tingle of pride at the fact that their son's talent had come to the notice of someone else outside of the community; but Black David knew that pride was a sin above all others. Mixed with the sense of pride was the thought of fear that their son, fast approaching his restless years, would be very tempted to try something like competition.

Black David himself had once—during the same years—participated in a competition, just to understand what it was like. During his Rumspringa, he had been given the chance to take part in a "home run contest" through the softball league, and had taken it. There had been a thrill as he hit one ball after another, driving them far out into the field; but the instant of recognition, and the good feeling it had brought with it, were nothing compared to the self-consciousness and the feeling of exposure that had come with winning the competition. Black David had not known what to do with himself as he stood there with the trophy. When he had taken his oath and been baptized, Black David had given the trophy to the parents of an

Englischer boy who was ill and could not participate in such tournaments—but dearly wished to be a baseball player.

Black David had always loved the Lord; even during his run-about years, he had not strayed very far from the teachings of the church. He had tasted alcohol, and had—once—sampled a puff of a marijuana cigarette, because he had been in the years of trying things. But he had never been tempted beyond his ability to overcome. Nothing in the Englischer world had enough glitter to compensate him for what he would be leaving behind: the solace of his community, the love of a good wife, the promise of a good life spent at hard work. He had trusted in the benign and loving words that he had learned from a young age all his life, and prayed.

They spoke for a little while about Barbara's sister; his wife cried a little more, but more gently, simply saying that she wished there could be a way to know that Salome was all right. That she was happy. It was difficult for Black David to be able to imagine that the woman who had left her community—left even her family, in accordance with the Meidung—could be completely contented in her new life. Rather than lie to his wife—which would be a sin—Black David merely kept his peace on the issue. He knew that Barbara wished, and even sometimes prayed, for a way to know whether or not her sister was well, whether Salome had found happiness. But there was no way of contacting those who had broken their vows. There was no way to know.

Black David hugged his wife tightly and kissed her forehead, and then her lips, the way that he always did when they were alone together and she needed comfort. "What God has ordained to happen will always happen," Black David told his wife. She nodded; it was cold comfort, he knew—but it was comfort nonetheless.

They would have to speak to their son. "We must make sure he understands the rules, that he knows of our concern for him," Black David said, and Barbara nodded agreement. "If that Englischer man spoke to him, we need to have everything in the clear, and understand what our son's thoughts on the matter are." Black David knew that it could be a temptation indeed; but he hoped that his son was not moved by the glittering gold of it. But the only way to know for sure would be to talk to the boy. Barbara cleaned her face and Black David and she went together to their son's room.

They knocked, knowing that the boy was reflecting quietly within. Though they were in charge of the home—and there could be no doubt otherwise—both of the Beilers respected the need for their children to have privacy, and waited to be allowed into their children's rooms, especially now that both son and daughter were of an age where they were reaching maturity. David called out that they could come in, after only a moment; that at least was exactly as it should be.

"Son, your Mamm and I wanted to talk to you for a moment," Black David said, glancing at his wife to make sure that she was as yet calm. Barbara was composed, her face bearing none—or at least very few—of the signs of her prolonged crying before.

"Is something wrong?" David asked, his young face twisting into a concerned frown. Black David resisted the urge to smile as he saw the fleeting resemblance between his son and his wife; in coloration and build, David was as like his father as any child could possibly be. But there were moments—flickers, rarer and rarer as the boy came of age—of the woman who had borne him. Just as their daughter was more and more like Barbara every day, David was more and more like Black David every day, but Black David still treasured those few flickers of resemblance the boy bore to his mother.

"You met an Englischer man on the road the other day, is that so?" Black David asked, sitting down at his son's desk. David shrugged.

"I did not go out of my way to meet him," he said. "He drove up on me in the road and stopped." Barbara nodded, and Black David recognized that their son was probably telling the truth.

"Did he speak with you?" Black David asked.

"I spoke with him after he saw you," Barbara explained. "When you came into the house." The younger David nodded.

"He said something about… about the Englischer high school, about joining a running team." David shrugged. Black

David frowned—only slightly. He was not angry with his son; he was irritated—a little—with the Englisch man.

"He asked you to join the running team?" Black David asked. His son hesitated only a moment before nodding.

"I told him nee, Daed. I ran away from him as quickly as I could without being rude." Black David caught the flash of a smile on his wife's face.

"You did as you should," Black David said. "What were your reasons for telling him you would not join?" Black David was curious; was it just that his son knew that it was forbidden, or did the younger David have his own understanding, his own reasons for knowing that it was a bad course of action? Black David watched as his son considered the question.

"I know that it is forbidden in the Ordnung," David said slowly. "It is not right to attempt to gain attention, or to set myself apart from others as special." Black David nodded, encouraging his son to continue. "I also know that we do not continue in school beyond the age of fourteen, or what the Englischers call eighth grade—so even if there were not the Ordnung against competition, I would not be able to join the team, because I could not be at the Englischer school." Barbara coughed softly.

"You are coming into the time of experimentation and restlessness," she pointed out to their son, and Black David saw the concern in his wife's eyes. "It—I fear that it could be a great temptation for you during your Rumspringa." Black David watched his son closely, wondering what was on the younger boy's mind. God had not given any man the ability to know what was in another's thoughts, in another's heart. His son may be saying the right things, but there was little way of knowing if he was only saying it to satisfy his parents and keep them from worrying, or of David really meant it.

"Mamm, you know I'm probably going to come right back to Bird-in-Hand when my Rumspringa is over," David said, shrugging off the idea of temptation. Black David felt a flicker of amusement—he had had much the similar notion when he had contemplated his Rumspringa. Of course, Black David *had* come back to the community when he had felt that he had learned all he needed to of the Englisch world, tasted all of the temptation he was interested in, and found it not as inviting as a good home, a good life, and a good family. And for the most part, the Amish who went out into the world a little bit came back at the end; eight or nine out of ten Amish youths could be expected to come home, take their oaths, and be baptized. But of course there were always a few, every year; and Barbara's sister was one of those who proved that even taking the oath did not always guarantee that someone would stay. Anna— Barbara's sister—was not the only one who had ever broken the oath and left the community; but she was the one closest to the family.

"I know that you think you know yourself," Black David said to his son slowly. Though he knew as David's father that he knew his son better—it was important to show some respect for the growing young man's efforts at self-reflection and development. "But there are many temptations in the world. It's impossible to say what choice you will make until the time comes to make it—and to think that you can know something like that is a mark of hubris." Black David said the words gently; he knew that youth was a time when even the most devout boy felt a little prideful. He also knew, however, that the lesson—and the warning—needed to be heeded, and that a small reproach now might save himself, Barbara, and even their son, a great deal of grief later.

CHAPTER FIVE

David was not unduly surprised when his evening reflections were interrupted by his parents' arrival at his room. He valued the privacy that he had, the time to himself—to think, to consider his lessons, do his homework when he had it—but he also knew that when his parents did want to speak to him, he should respect them and allow them into his room without hesitation. An honest boy, who loved God, David always considered that he had nothing—or at least very little—to hide from his parents.

He felt a flash of guilt as he discussed the Englischer man with his father and mother; he told them, honestly, that he had told the sports teacher that he would not join the team, and had explained his meeting with the man and why he had responded the way he had. But he did not tell them the little flash of excitement he had felt at the thought of the possibility of competition. He did not tell them anything about his thoughts of how it would be possible to try—to get just a little taste—during his Rumspringa, and just know what it was like.

In part, David did not mention these things to his parents because he didn't want to worry them; he knew if he told them about those thoughts, they would be concerned at the possibility of him acting on them. David also knew that he wasn't quite sure that he wouldn't; but he knew that for the moment, the idea of courting Salome was more important to him than any possibility of competition or what the Englischers considered so important: glory.

Conflicted thoughts plagued him; David reassured his mother, knowing that she worried not only for the possibility of losing her son, but because she had totally lost her eldest sister, David's aunt Anna. While the Meidung meant that nobody could talk to her, and if she came back into the community without repenting of having broken her oath, nobody could take anything from her—though if she was in need, they could provide aid—everyone in the little community knew about the sad story of her departure. The way it had torn apart his mother's family, the fact that Barbara still mourned, never able to know how her sister fared—it was common knowledge.

And David felt secure enough in his future, after thinking of Salome Lapp, that he could reassure his Mamm that he had absolutely no intentions whatsoever of having anything to do with the Englischer running team. It seemed—as he talked to his parents more and more—to be ridiculous even to him; the temptation lost its luster little by little as they described it and talked about it. Why running was something that a person could compete with seemed beyond understanding; running was something that most people could do at least a little bit. When survival demanded it, even those who could normally not run at all often managed to find at least a small reserve of ability to get up and move quickly. David knew that it was something of a talent that he had—there was no false modesty required. Whether it was worthwhile to concern himself with it; that was the question. That, David was not sure of. But he understood that his parents were worried for him, and he told his Mamm that she had nothing to worry about; that he was happy in their community. "I'm happy to learn at Daed's side," he said. "I love to work hard, and I love knowing more and more about carpentry. It's a good, important job, and it always needs doing."

"I'm glad to hear you saying that, son," Black David said, smiling with something that was not quite pride in his dark eyes. "It's good that you understand the importance of work and of each job that a man can do; we can't be farmers, our family: land is too costly, and after a few generations, we're not made for it anymore. But we can do our part to help the community continue to exist."

"And we make a living," David said, quietly but firmly. Part of the work that Black David did—a large part, in fact, which the younger David helped out with—was for Englischers who wanted Amish-made cabinetry and furniture.

It wasn't only buildings that Black David helped to make but finished goods, and that was something that everyone always seemed to need; a trunk, or a cabinet, a table and set of chairs, bed frames, desks. There was always more work to do, always something else that needed to be made.

"Yes, we do—though you're too young to understand the need to know the difference between wanting to make enough to live and wanting to make money for it's own sake." David bristled instinctively at that. He knew that his father did not mean his words in a haughty or mean way; but there was something in him, some restlessness, some confidence that was not-quite-pride, that disliked being told that he was too young to know something, even if he understood, objectively, that he was still very young, with much of life ahead of him. He conquered the feeling and listened to his parents' counsel.

After a while, it became clear that David's protestations of wanting to remain in the community and wanting to take his oath when he had gone through Rumspringa were enough to satisfy his parents. "I'm glad that you have good, sound reasons for having done the right thing," his mother said, smiling with the warmth that he loved in her. "When you know why you're doing something—that's just as important as knowing to do it in the first place."

"Like knowing how to measure properly," Black David added with a wry grin.

"I know that right now you're on the right track of things," David's mother said. "I can only hope and pray that you'll continue to have a good understanding, and make right choices." By the time the conversation had ended, it was very nearly time for David to go to sleep; the events of the day had left him almost completely exhausted, and he was glad when his parents rose to leave—not because he didn't enjoy their presence and counsel, but because his bed seemed like a siren itself, calling him to strip down out of his day clothes, into his nightshirt, and slide down underneath the blankets.

David took the time to carefully make sure he had everything he would need for the next day after his parents took their leave, and he washed his face, his hands, and his neck; he brushed his teeth and hair, and then undressed for the night before climbing into his bed. In spite of the fact that he had told his parents in no uncertain terms that the prospect of competition did not tempt him as much as future, stable happiness, David's mind swirled with points and counterpoints, possibilities and almost-dreams of what could be. He fell into sleep almost without warning, between one thought and the next.

CHAPTER SIX

"Did you hear about the Englischer sports coach who wants David Beiler to join some running team?" Salome looked at her friend in surprise as they both walked back from the general store together, carrying purchases their respective mothers had requested. She felt the heat rising into her cheeks at the mention of David Beiler but shook her head, trying to pretend that she had only a passing curiosity in the news. "I don't understand it, but I heard it from my sister—she's friends with David's sister." Anne, Salome's friend, lived closer to the Beiler family than Salome and her mother did; as a result, she often had better news of the family's events.

"Well, he is very good at running," Salome said. "I mean— not that I—I don't watch him, but we've all seen him running here and there." She felt her cheeks warming even more and changed the subject to something that would allow her to keep her composure.

Even still, as they both walked back towards the little complex of homes and farms, Salome's mind whirled. She had, in fact, watched David running—though not out of any sense of carnality, just in curiosity and amazement at the ability he had. Everyone in the community knew that David could run fast, and for a long time. He had been at it since they had all been little more than babies; it wasn't as though it was a secret for anyone.

Part of Salome's mind insisted that David would have no interest in such things. From what she knew of him—from being in school together, meeting each other at Sings after church services, speaking when it was possible and proper to talk in groups of youth their own age—Salome thought that David was far too devout, far too dedicated to his future as a member of the community, to want to take part in something like a competition.

Unlike her friend Anne, Salome knew much more about the Englischer world; she paid attention in school and sometimes—though she felt guilty about it afterwards— eavesdropped on conversations between Englisch men and women when she was running errands for her mother. She knew about the high school, small as it was, and she knew about the sports teams. If somehow David could be persuaded to join the high school in spite of the Ordnung, then he would definitely be eligible to compete—and he might, Salome thought, just be restless enough, intrigued enough, tempted enough, to join the high school, against the rules of their community as it was.

As Salome and Anne parted ways for each of them to return to their separate houses, Salome considered the news as it concerned David. While Salome would have liked to have thought that David was impervious to such a temptation, she knew that no one was truly impervious to temptation. There had always been members of the community who found themselves unable to resist and broke their oaths, or who found themselves punished because they had broken with the Ordnung.

Nothing had been said between them—and indeed, Salome knew all too well that nothing could be said between them for some time to come—but she had cherished a tender regard for David for years; since he had defended her from an Englischer boy who had tried to bully her in one of the shops. David had managed to convince the boy to stand down and leave her alone without resorting to violence, standing firm and watching as he left. From that point forward, Salome had tried to do what she could to talk to David—little as that could be, especially as they gradually came of age. The possibility that David could end up forever out of reach, leaving the community for the glitter of competition (for Salome had no doubt that with David's extraordinary abilities, he would be what the Englischers called "a star"), and leaving her alone.

She considered what she could do. *I could tell Anne stories about things that happen to runners sometimes—injuries and things—and maybe she would tell David's sister, who would tell him...* Salome thought. Or she could be a little more open about her affection for David, and maybe—maybe—inspire him to focus on the certainty of a good future instead of the allure of a possibility. Her mind ticked through ways that she could go about dissuading the boy she cared about from leaving the community, from breaking with the Ordnung, but even as she thought of each one, Salome realized the futility; she would not be doing right to tell lies to someone, even in a good cause. She knew that it would bring trouble not only on her but also on her mother if she were more open in her affections for David, since they were both too young to court. Any form of subterfuge or scheme was forbidden for one very good reason or another, and as Salome approached her house, she sighed.

She decided as she reflected on the trouble that the only proper, right, commendable thing to do would be to pray to God about it, and hope that God would lead David into the right path, to stay with the people who knew him and cared about him, instead of falling into the temptations of the Englischer world. David had free will, and could make mistakes as he must—but Salome had to hope that God would give him the ability to make the best possible choice. She stopped short at the front porch of the house that she shared with her mother and closed her eyes, taking a deep breath and silently reciting a prayer to God. It was the best—and ultimately the only—thing she could do.

CHAPTER SEVEN

Black David alighted from his buggy in the yard of Ruth and Samuel King's house on Sunday morning, feeling contented as he always did that it was a meeting day and there would be church to attend. He was equally contented on the alternate Sundays when the order of the day was either to visit family and friends or to take a rest at home. Somehow, the troubles of the week melted away at least for the few quiet hours of the day on Sundays, and Black David was able to think of them more clearly the following day, refreshed by his repose.

He spotted several of his friends as their families pulled into the yard at the Kings' house, and nodded to them with a faint smile on his face. Black David looked around and realized that nearly everyone had either arrived or was pulling up along the road to come into the yard; the meeting would start soon. He saw that his son was just as energetic as ever, mingling amongst his friends in a mixed group of youth his age—boys and girls both. Black David looked around more and spotted Bishop Fisher; at his side was Mark Schrock, a lay minister who was popular in the community and who had worked out well in spite of a little trepidation at his election to the post. Before the meeting began, Black David wanted to talk to both men; he did not want to put the task off until after the meeting, which would—as always, and joyously—be hours in duration.

"Good morning to you, Black David," Tom Fisher said, inclining his head towards David in greeting. Black David shook hands with the Bishop and with Mark.

"Good morning to you both. It's a fine one for a meeting day." They spoke for a few moments quietly, glancing every now and then around them to see that their wives were moving about, that the children were playing quietly, little murmurs of contentment in their midst. Finally Black David came to the purpose of his move to speak to the two men.

He told the Bishop and Mark about what had come to pass; about David's running prowess being witnessed by an Englischer sports teacher, how Barbara had sent the man away when he had suggested that David could join the team. "Did she explain to him why it was that your son could not join?" the Bishop asked. Black David shook his head slowly.

"She told him firmly that David would not be joining the team, that he could not." The Bishop nodded, frowning but not in reproof.

"If he comes again—and you know he may, to speak with you as the boy's father, it would be good to explain to him that the rules of our community do not allow us to join in competition," the Bishop said. Mark nodded his agreement, and Black David felt a little bit better.

"It's possible that once he knows about our Ordnung, he will understand," Mark suggested.

"Keep an eye on your son, of course," Tom said, glancing in the direction of the younger David Beiler. "He's at an age when temptations are many and self-control is little. I would guard against him having any time to speak to the Englischer man alone." Black David nodded his agreement.

"Just as you say," David said, looking from one man to the other. "He's going to deal with enough temptation in his life without something like this included."

"Do you think he's started to think of courting?" Black David smiled.

"As much as any boy his age thinks about it—I don't know his preference for certain, but I've seen him color up around Salome Lapp." Mark started , recovering after only an instant.

"Well if he is interested in courting, then the odds are likely that he will remain true to his word and stay among us," Mark said smoothly. Black David had described the conversation with his son that he and his wife had had as quickly as the subject would allow.

"I hope to God he makes the right decision," Black David said. The Bishop nodded.

"That is the best thing that most of us can do: hope and pray to God, and take the most reasonable possible precautions against harm." It was nearly time to go into the house where the meeting would be, and Black David parted from the ministers with good feelings in his heart, thinking that at least he could put the thought of his son and the Englischer coach aside for several hours during the prayers and songs of the day's service.

CHAPTER EIGHT

John King could smell the scents of a good meal on the air as the meeting broke up; but hungry as he was after hours of worship, his interest was not in the food that his cousins' house boasted—the combined efforts of several women in the community—but in one of those who would be serving the meal to the men before taking her place at the women's table. It would be unseemly to appear as though he was looking for any woman in particular, but John King thought that if he was discreet, there was nothing wrong in noticing someone.

Sarah Lapp's soft-featured, fine face appeared amongst the rest of the women who came to serve the men's table, and John King watched her, though he did not betray any sign that he had noticed her; no flicker of interest, no twitch of his lips, made any indication that he was doing anything other than waiting for the big communal meal to begin. He carefully scrutinized her in careful glances: her blonde hair was concealed underneath a firmly-tied bonnet, her clothing was neat and clean, covering her arms to her wrist and her legs to almost the tops of her feet, showing her to be appropriately modest and humble. As she passed behind him, John King could smell the faint scent of the lavender and cedar sachet she used in her drawers and closets, mingling with the warm smells of bread and baking.

All in all, John decided, Sarah Lapp would make a very appropriate wife for him. Though it pained him to have to look for a new wife, as a minister within the community, John knew that he needed to model the life of a responsible man. That meant that he would need to have a wife. Because he was older—well past his Rumspringa, and because he was already a widower, the courtship process would be very different. *We are not so different from each other,* he thought as he made the decision to bide his time; adult or not, member of the community or not—and widower or not—it would not be in keeping with the Ordnung for him to approach Sarah at a time like this. He would speak with her privately another time. *She is a widow, I am a widower. We both need a spouse—she even more than I, with her daughter coming up.*

But John knew that he would have to bide his time. He would enjoy the meal, enjoy the fellowship of his community, and exchange a few words with Sarah later; while his courtship with her would not be as lengthy or as involved as it would were he and Sarah both still young, there were certain forms that would have to be obeyed. He was not about to raise a scandal. John thought about his late wife briefly; he could wish very deeply that there would be no need for him to find another wife, and he felt the pain of her loss and the misfortune that came with it. Perhaps, he thought, there was still time for him to have children. If nothing else, Salome Lapp would need fatherly guidance now more than ever—she was entering the season of high spirits, almost the age to have her Rumspringa. Now, more than ever, she would need a firm hand, mature minds to keep her in line.

Before long, the meal had ended, and it was nearly time for the adults to retire to their homes, leaving the boys and girls to their evening Sing. John stood; he had no reason to linger, but he found his way over to the women's table where Sarah Lapp sat, talking contentedly with the other women. He nearly lost his nerve—he was unaccustomed to speaking with women, after his marriage and after the loss of his wife and the mourning that followed it. But John King paused at the table. "Good afternoon, Sarah Lapp," he said, inclining his head gravely towards her. "I am glad to see you for worship today." Sarah looked up at him, startled, and a surprisingly maidenly blush came over her face, as her dark brown eyes flickered with confused surprise.

"It is good to see you too, John," Sarah said quickly.

"I trust that you and your daughter are both well?" John glanced around, looking for Salome and unable to spot her. Sarah nodded, looking at the other women at the table, who had gone almost silent in mild surprise that John had stopped to speak with anyone. John forced a smile to curve his lips.

"Yes, we are," Sarah said, smiling as well. "Thank you for asking after us."

"I hope I will see you again soon," John said, inclining his head once more. He hesitated, wanting to say something more but uncertain of what he should say. He looked around at the other women, talking amongst themselves, and took his leave, giving Sarah Lapp a brief smile as he turned to go.

After he reached his silent home, John sat quietly in his kitchen for a few moments, considering what to do to spend the rest of the afternoon and the evening. He knew already that he would go to bed early; he had nothing to keep him awake. There were a few necessary chores to attend to around the house—nothing that would violate the rule of keeping the Sabbath day holy. With no wife or child, he had few reasons to visit his neighbors. He contemplated his life and decided once more that of all of the possible options for a wife within his community, Sarah Lapp made the most sense. John did not want to partner with a young woman who was just past the flighty, rambunctious years, someone who he would have to watch for and remind. A woman of experience was the best choice, and Sarah Lapp was appropriately modest, humble, and steady. John sighed, moving to check on the animals—the horses in their stalls, the couple of cows who might need to be milked, the chickens.

It would be good, too, John thought, to have help around his farm. Though he was determined to maintain his home and lands industriously, it was sometimes taxing, and a wife who could be a helpmeet was welcome. John checked on his animals, making sure that their feed containers were full enough, that they were resting comfortably—after all, the Sabbath was a day of rest for animals as well as humans. As he headed back, he decided that he would definitely make the opportunity to speak with Sarah about the possibility of courting. "After all, it is time," he said to himself in the quiet of his home, settling down to a meal of cold leftover meat and cheese and bread.

CHAPTER NINE

Sarah Lapp sat, watching the flickering of moths outside in the light of her porch lantern. It had been a good Sabbath; worship had given her the sense of peace that it always did, and opportunities to speak with her friends and relatives made her happy. She sipped at her coffee, thinking to herself that Salome should be coming home from the Sing soon, and her thoughts turned onto the subject of John King.

Why would he mark me out by speaking to me in particular? It troubled Sarah for reasons she wasn't entirely sure she could name to herself that John in particular had spoken to her. She knew that he had lost his wife fairly recently—there had been whispers in the community, and John's wife had died so suddenly, with no one entirely certain of how. John had always been a quiet, self-contained kind of man, as Sarah remembered; but he also had something of a— she couldn't quite call it nosy, but something unsettling, a kind of watchful gaze and a tendency to comment that she wasn't sure she liked.

Sarah had been widowed for two years; she felt a jolt of sadness at the memory of her husband's passing. Her husband had been a gentle, kind man, humble before God and patient with others' frailties. Sarah smiled to herself sadly. After two years, with a daughter who was on the point of adulthood—and years of childbearing left to her—Sarah knew that it was high time to find another husband. The thought that John King might have his eye on her for a wife was somewhat unsettling. *Surely not,* Sarah thought, shaking her head. *He thought to speak to me for whatever reasons he might have, but surely he hasn't already decided who he would like to marry next.*

But would it be so bad if John King were interested in courting her? He had a farm, and to the best of Sarah's knowledge, he was a productive and industrious man. John was a minister of the Church; she thought that he would therefore be a good moral figure for her daughter to look up to. Thoughts of John's wife's sudden death were less than comforting—but surely if there had been any truly suspicious circumstances, John would have been subject to the Meidung, and turned into the Englischer authorities. No; he must be a righteous and humble man. Perhaps a little colder than some of the other men of the Bird-in-Hand community, but that didn't mean that he was a bad man.

Before she went to bed, Sarah closed her eyes in prayer. If her suspicion was true—if John King were interested in courting her—then she hoped for God's guidance as to whether or not to accept him. He seemed cold; but he might not be. "Perhaps he is simply one of those who needs to know what others are doing," Sarah said out loud, opening her eyes as she finished her silent prayer. "He also seems so quiet and kind." She silently asked once more that God would guide her steps, would make the right choice clear to her. Sarah cleaned her coffee mug and banked the kitchen fire embers so that the house would be warm for Salome to return to at the end of the Sing. She went to bed having resolutely reminded herself of the Gospel of Matthew's advice, "Take therefore no thought for the morrow: for the morrow shall take thought for the things of itself. Sufficient unto the day is the evil thereof."

CHAPTER TEN

Several weeks later, Sarah had put the matter firmly out of her mind; after a few days, she had reasoned that if John King had intentions of asking to court her, he would approach her directly and quickly. Her life was full of wholesome and satisfying work, and now that Salome was finishing her schooling and entering into her quilting apprenticeship, Sarah had her own daughter's continued education to consider as well as her normal tasks. Salome's growing expertise in sewing meant that Sarah's load was lightened—but it also meant that she could take on more work. Between her livelihood and the ongoing tasks needed to keep her home running, Sarah had little time to worry about things that might never happen.

She even began to view her previous concern about John, about his wife, and the prospect of courting again so soon as somewhat silly. John King's wife had not been dead for very long; surely he was not looking to marry again so soon. It was barely appropriate for her after two years.

Sarah was seated in the living room, mending one of Salome's dresses by the fire's light. Salome, her daughter, had already gone to bed; but Sarah found that without a husband to warm her own bed, to offer companionship in the dark nights, she was more inclined to stay up a little later, getting to the few things she never seemed to be able to fit into the day. She rocked back and forth in the chair her husband's skilled hands had built for her early in their marriage, meditative and quietly contented as her needle moved in and out of the fabric in the deft, steady movements that came from years of practice.

Her thoughts were interrupted by the sound of a sharp, short series of raps on her front door. Startled, Sarah set her mending immediately aside and rose from the rocking chair all in one movement. It was well after dark; she could only imagine that there was some emergency—that one of her friends might be sick, or one of the men might be injured, and someone needed for her to watch their children for the evening, or assist in some way. Sarah's heart beat faster in her chest as she walked the dozen steps from the den to the front door of the house, pulling her bonnet on quickly.

Instead of a friend or member of the community come to offer bad news, as Sarah Lapp opened the door, she saw none other than John King standing there, looking grave but not alarmed. "I apologize for the late hour, Sarah," he said, nodding . "But I wanted the opportunity to speak to you in private." Sarah stared at him for a moment in shock, uncertain of how, exactly, she should react. If she had been her daughter's age it would be unthinkable for a single man to enter her home at night—even if she had never been married, it would be inappropriate.

But she was a widow; the rules were not quite the same, and perhaps John had something important to tell her. Sarah opened the door a little more widely to admit her late caller and gestured for him to go into the kitchen. "I may have some bread or pie left from the evening meal," she said quietly.

"That would be welcome," John told her as she closed the door silently behind him. He gave her a slight, stilted smile that had little warmth in it at all, and Sarah made herself return it.

Sarah busied herself in the kitchen, feeling self-conscious about the fact that there was a single man—even if he was a widower—in her home after dark. She brewed coffee and offered John a slice of apple pie and some bread and cheese before sitting down with a cup of her own, feeling flustered. "I hope I didn't startle you too much," John said, taking a sip of coffee.

"I wasn't expecting anyone," Sarah replied, and then smiled. "But an unexpected visit from a friend can be pleasant." John returned her smile, though it did not quite meet his bright blue eyes.

"I'm glad you see me as your friend," John told her. "I know that your husband has not been away from you for very long; nor has my wife." Sarah nodded.

"We've both of us felt loss," she said, agreeing with him.

"I was hoping that you might have turned your thoughts towards finding a new husband." Sarah brought her coffee mug up to her lips to cover the slight shock she felt.

"I have thought about it," she admitted after a moment.

"We're both without the companionship we need," John pointed out. "And since you have a daughter, just coming into her rambunctious years… I thought perhaps you wouldn't find it too forward of me to ask if I could court you." Sarah swallowed a bite of bread, barely chewing it.

"I'm not sure, John," Sarah admitted. "Salome and I have become very close, and while I will admit that I am sometimes lonely…" she set her mug down.

"I have seen the loneliness in you," John told her, and for the first time she saw real emotion in his eyes. "I have felt it myself. You are a godly woman, humble and modest, and as soon as I turned my thoughts towards starting my life anew, I thought of you." Sarah took another sip of her coffee.

"We do not know each other well," Sarah said, thinking of the rumors of John's first wife, and the uncertainties she had felt on the subject of courting in general.

"What else is courting for, if not to get to know each other?" John pointed out. Sarah had to agree to his assertion.

They spoke for over an hour, with John telling Sarah about the life that he could offer her; she would want for nothing— he could support her and Salome on his own, and her industriousness would keep them both comfortable. John spoke of his desire to have children, and Sarah had to admit that she herself, as Salome came closer to being an adult, felt the desire for another child to raise. By the time John bid her a good night to return to his home, Sarah found herself agreeing—if a little reluctantly—to accept his advances, to get to know him better with an eye towards possibly becoming his wife. There would be little formality; neither of them was young. But for the time being, they would simply be getting to know each other. Sarah went to bed confused about her feelings, but with softer, kinder sensations towards John King. *Perhaps this is a sign from God,* she thought as she went through her house, making sure that the kitchen fire was banked, the den fire down to embers that would die slowly. Sarah climbed into her bed and went to sleep with a mostly untroubled mind.

CHAPTER ELEVEN

Sarah told herself as she started her courtship with John that she needn't think too seriously about it. After all, at thirty-three years of age, while she could still have another child, she had become accustomed to the idea of living alone with her daughter. Salome would begin her own courting in two years' time, when she was of age, but Sarah thought that it would be restful to live completely on her own. So as she and John began to keep company, Sarah reminded herself that she could decide not to marry him; it would not be unseemly, or cruel.

But over time, she saw that John did not have a similarly light attitude towards their courtship. As he was driving her home from Worship one Sunday afternoon, John asked her, "How long do you think you will need to get to know me before you feel comfortable with the idea of being my wife?" Sarah had been thoroughly nonplussed by the question, and a hasty suggestion that if he wanted a ready wife, he should speak with some of the younger women of the community rose to her lips, only to be defeated by a more patient thought.

"I am afraid I don't know, John," Sarah said. "I do not want either of us to be unequally yoked; we should get to know each other very well. After all, we have time." John had gone silent at that, for the rest of the ride from the site of the Church for that week, but when he stopped at her home, offering her assistance in getting down from the buggy, he finally spoke once more.

"I would like to see you as often as possible, so that we can get to know each other better." Sarah had agreed to see him again soon, though the directness of his comment bothered her for reasons she could not quite bring herself to name.

The next week, John and Sarah sat on her front porch, drinking coffee and talking. "I noticed the other day," John said abruptly, glancing at Sarah, "That Salome lifted the hem of her dress a little too high as she was walking back through the puddles earlier this week."

"I'm sure she didn't do it intentionally," Sarah pointed out, smiling politely. John's face turned grave.

"Intentionally or not, you must speak with her. Accidental immodesty is the path to intentional immodesty. Salome is still very young; she must start in the habits of mindfulness now." Sarah had started to counter that even God could overlook an accident, but the seriousness of John's face, of his voice, told her that it would be a bad idea. She had agreed to speak to Salome about her lapse.

She and John went to dinner in the Englischer town, choosing a modest diner, and she learned from John that she herself was not without unintentional outrages against modesty and propriety. As she sat herself down, she could feel the cool air brush the skin just above her ankle—and she felt her bonnet slide back just slightly. John had hissed, "Do not make a temptation of yourself, Sarah," and she had quickly corrected the fall of her dress, had straightened her bonnet. After a few minutes, John had begun to relax—but there was something about his tight-voiced, sharp criticism that stayed with her nonetheless.

As they got to know each other better, over weeks and months, Sarah's mind went back and forth on the subject of whether or not to continue her courtship with John. Sometimes, he seemed kind, gentle, quiet and patient; qualities that any woman would want in the man she would marry. But other times, he seemed cold—and in addition to his sharp criticisms, she found that he was more than commonly interested in what she was doing.

Two months into their courtship, John began coming by her home several times a week; he said that he simply wanted to check on her, and make sure her day was progressing well. But he would ask minute questions about where Salome was, what Sarah was doing, who she was visiting. When she missed one of his calls to her house due to an emergency at her cousin's farm, John had reproached her sharply for failing to tell him—her potential future husband—where she would be. "You did not even leave a note for me. You did not send Salome to tell me where you were going."

Sarah apologized for her lapses as best as she could, reasoning that John would not be so concerned if he did not care deeply for her. She spoke with some of her friends, cautiously, about the fact that she was courting John; the soft silences of the women whose opinions she had come to value made Sarah more than a little uneasy; but she told herself again and again that she had good reasons to continue to value John's companionship and interest in her.

One evening, John was driving her home from the Englischer town where she had dropped off several quilts she had made for sale, and Sarah found herself conflicted. "John," she said quietly, looking at her hands in her lap, at the floor of the buggy that her potential future husband drove them both in. "I can see that you are very serious about courting me, but I am not sure I know you much better than when we started." She glanced at him, feeling an instinctive fear that she told herself was silly.

"I think that we are getting to know each other quite well," John said with something like contentment. "I feel more and more that you're a woman I can spend the rest of my life with."

"I'm…" Sarah took a deep breath. Her heart was beating faster and faster in her chest. "I'm concerned with how you scolded Salome this morning when you saw her running up the road."

"She was being immodest," John said firmly. "I scolded her because I knew that you had not seen it."

"I do not think it was so bad as you might have thought," Sarah said, biting her bottom lip as words threatened to come pouring out.

"It's important to root these things out before they become larger sins," John told her.

"Why are you—why are you so concerned? No human is perfect, John. We are all born with the taint of original sin." John's lips turned down in a sharp frown.

"I strive to become a better man every day; if you become my wife, I would expect for you and Salome both to strive to become better women every day. If you do not know when you are erring, how can you improve?" Sarah swallowed against the dryness she felt in her throat.

"That is reasonable," she said quietly. "But I wonder sometimes if there might be a reason that you feel... that you need to be so firm. So—I do not wish to call you cold, but sometimes your manner is icy." John was silent for a long time.

"My mother was... sometimes unreliable. She was good of heart, but I learned that I could not depend on her." John lapsed into quietness for another long moment. "I want to do everything I can to remedy the faults she bequeathed to me."

"But John," Sarah said, looking at the man that she very much wanted to love and trust, in spite of her misgivings. "I think—perhaps—that you might be prone to overcorrect."

"I do no more than my duty as a minister, as a man who seeks to be in line with what God desires for his creation," John told her stiffly. Sarah decided that there was no reason to continue the topic.

"I would appreciate it if, in future, you would bring your concerns about Salome to me," she said quietly. "You may become her Daed at some point, but right now—and always—I am her Mam. If anyone is to discipline her right now, it should be me."

"She should become accustomed to discipline from me," John said, his face forming grave, solemn lines. "But I will consider your suggestion." Sarah saw his expression soften, and told herself that no man—no matter how haunted he might be, no matter how deep in grief—was beyond reaching, if he wanted to be good. She put aside her misgivings once more and continued her courtship with John, thinking that if they could come to a few agreements, that she could love him with all her heart, the way that a wife should.

CHAPTER TWELVE

With school ending for summer, Salome found her days both busier than before and yet also calmer. Her mother gave her more tasks as her apprentice—she was now stitching together some of the smaller portions of quilts for a few hours a day, piecing them so that her mother could bring them together into the intricate overall patterns that the quilts would eventually take—but because she was no longer spending hours of the day in school, and running more errands for her mother, Salome could spend more time with her friends. "You are a young woman," her mother had told her smilingly. "It is not yet time for you to start looking for a husband, but you deserve some freedom." It pleased Salome most of all that she had earned her mother's trust; Sarah knew that Salome would not err, and while Salome tried to avoid a sense of wrongful pride, she couldn't help but be happy that she had shown herself to be trustworthy.

Summer brought with it all kinds of social occasions; sports for the children of the community, Sings, building parties, and visiting. Once her chores and duties were done, Salome found herself meeting up with friends—Miriam Fisher, Martha King, her cousin Ruth Lapp. Because she was coming into adulthood, even if she was not quite of age yet, Salome had few restrictions; her mother pushed her to go to any socials she wanted to attend, to go to softball or volleyball games, to join teams.

Salome was not the only one in her age group with more freedom with the coming of summer; she tried to avoid making too much of a note of it, but she saw David Beiler more and more frequently. Salome was careful never to spend any time with David alone if she could avoid it—the watchful gaze of John King seemed to extend everywhere, and any trust she had earned from her Mamm would evaporate if there was a scandal against her—but she couldn't help occasionally looking at David as they spent time in groups together, meeting his gaze and giving him a little smile. She didn't quite dare to say more than the most casual things, simple hellos and small talk; but Salome felt a little tingle of warmth every time she was in a group with David.

She also couldn't help but think that David wished to be closer to her as well. Every time they met, he returned her smile, his cheeks coloring pink, his bright eyes dancing with an emotion that Salome couldn't quite read. She felt her heart beating faster and wished that she dared to speak to him alone, even knowing that it would be "unseemly," as John King would call it. But there was a feeling like an insatiable curiosity that filled Salome. She still had hopes that perhaps, when they were both of the age to begin courting, David would think of her; he was so kind, so gentle and patient, and handsome. Occasionally, she remembered the incident months before when an Englischer running coach had offered him the chance to join the high school running team, but Salome had turned that matter over to God, and told herself whenever the thought intruded that it was as God willed.

For now, she would focus her efforts on getting to know David as best as she could, and spending time with her friends and cousins while she had the freedom. Salome knew that she could not say anything in particular about a preference, and she should get to know the boys as well as the young women of her community; though her eyes saw David the most favorably, her Mamm had counseled her more than once to take her time, to get to know everyone. "It is not for you to start choosing yet. There may be someone you like better in a few years when it's courting time. You will be spending the rest of your life with these people—you should know them well."

Salome went to a boys' softball game with Ruth and Martha and Miriam; she knew that David would be there, which she told herself was not the only reason to go. The other girls in the community who had finished their chores gathered to sit in the shade next to the softball diamond, chattering about their younger brothers and sisters, their work, the next social.

"My Mamm is teaching me about bringing babies," Ruth Beiler said in a hushed whisper. "She says in a few more weeks, if Martha King goes into labor, I can attend." There was a murmur of excitement through the girls. At fourteen, they knew only the very most basic things about being a woman; Salome remembered with a shiver the first time she had had her monthly course. Ruth's mother was a midwife, so Ruth knew a little bit more than any of the other girls about the mechanics of making and birthing babies.

The other girls peppered Ruth with questions and comments. "What do you think it will be like?" "My Mamm says she never screamed so much as when she was giving birth to my brother." Salome hung back, watching as the boys broke up into teams, barely paying attention to the conversation. She spotted David; he was always in the outfield because of his special running ability. John was one of the pitchers—he had joked that during his Rumspringa, he might see about joining a non-Amish team—and Samuel, another of the boys in her class at the school, played catcher for the same team as David and John. They started to play, and the girls turned their attention onto the field, cheering on their friends. Salome smiled privately to herself as she noticed David looking in her direction.

He nearly missed a long-drive hit looking at her—only called out of it at the last moment by a shout from one of the other boys on his team. Salome giggled softly to herself, bowing her head so that no one would see her. A little thrill of excitement crackled along her spine at the thought of David being so absorbed in watching her and the other girls talking that he had nearly lost the thread of the game. But she made herself take her attention away from only David and towards her friends and the two teams as a whole. "David Beiler almost missed his catch," Martha commented, giving Salome a nudge.

"He's got his head in the clouds like all of the boys," Salome said, smiling broadly. The boys didn't keep track too seriously of the points; the game was for fun. As the two teams played on, Salome took part in the conversations humming around her.

"Is your mother really courting with John King?" Miriam asked her quietly. Salome shrugged.

"I don't know if they are serious, but she did say that they are courting." The thought of that particular member of the community filled Salome with a kind of low dread. She had thought—as her mother had—that John King was a quiet, gentle kind of man, but as her Mamm and John had started to see each other more seriously, more and more of the man's nature came out. She shivered, hoping that something would change between them—either that John and her Mamm would decide that they did not want to be together, or that John's stern nature might soften.

The game ended with David's team winning, and the boys and girls came together to head back to the center of the community. It was midafternoon; Salome realized that her mother would want her to help with dinner, especially if John King was planning on coming to visit. But there was time for a leisurely stroll from the fields.

"Hi, Salome," David said, walking up beside her.

"Hello, David," Salome said, feeling her cheeks warm up with a blush. "That was a very good game."

"It was," David said, smiling. "You play volleyball, don't you?" Salome nodded.

"I'm on a team with Martha and Ruth and a few others," she agreed. "We're going to play again probably tomorrow, if Ruth can get away."

"If my Daed and I finish up with the orders, I'd love to watch you play." Salome felt her cheeks warming even more.

"I would like that a lot." She tried to think of something to say, but her heart was beating so fast, and her mind seemed to be utterly blank. She swallowed against the tight, dry feeling in her throat. "Do you like working with your Daed?"

"I really do," David said, looking away for a moment. "It's very interesting work."

"And you get to do all his errands," Salome pointed out with a grin. "Lots of opportunities to run." David laughed.

"Daed yelled at me the other day for running with some tools. I have to walk unless it's something that won't break or injure me."

"That must be difficult!" Salome giggled. She felt as if tiny butterflies were fluttering just beneath her skin. "No wonder you like playing softball so much. You get all of the running out of your system." David nodded.

"I think I may try playing soccer in the fall, if my Daed doesn't need me too much to practice. More running in that." Salome laughed; it was obvious to anyone who knew David even a little bit that he would take any excuse to run—soccer would be an excellent outlet for it. Her thoughts turned to the rumor about the Englischer coach, but while the Bird-in-Hand community was close-knit, Salome's family was not close enough with David's family for her to be able to comment on it. She said a silent prayer in her mind once more that David would be led away from the temptation to leave the community and the Church.

David speaking once more interrupted her thoughts. "Do you like learning with your Mamm? She is very good with her work." Salome found herself almost giggling at the fact that David seemed to have even noticed something like quilting.

"I am learning a great deal from her, and also from Ruth Fisher. Mamm says that Ruth has forgotten more about quilting than she will ever know." David smiled.

"That's what Daed says about some of the older men in the carpentry shop, too." For a few more blissful minutes, Salome and David discussed their apprenticeships, with David asking questions about how quilting worked, and Salome listening to his descriptions of careful measuring, sanding, and shaping of wood. Salome was pleased that David had such a strong interest in his future vocation; she thought—to herself, very quietly—that his enjoyment of the good, wholesome work would be an excellent way to keep him from following the path of temptation during his restless years.

But she knew that if she spoke too long to David, or to any of the boys, word would somehow get back to John King, and she would be in trouble both with him and with her Mamm. Salome reluctantly let the conversation between her and David die off, speeding up her steps to catch up to her closer friends in their group.

She tried to talk to some of the others, to avoid seeming like she was distinguishing David. But every step she took, Salome was aware of how close David was to her, aware of every movement he made in the corner of her vision. All too soon, the group of teenagers had reached the center of the community, and while Salome wished that she could linger with her friends, she knew that her Mamm would want her to help with dinner. Some of the others suggested that they could continue their walk into a hike, but Salome demurred. "My Mamm will want me to help her with the meal," she said, smiling sadly. She took her leave of her friends and started back towards the house she shared with her mother.

Salome's happy thoughts were marred by the expectation that John King would possibly be coming over for supper. She had known very little about John when he and her Mamm had started courting; John had always been a quiet kind of man, somewhat removed from the community even before his wife's sudden passing. Salome had heard the murmurs about how quickly John's wife had died—but it was unthinkable that he could have done anything to harm the woman he loved.

After a few months, however, it had become clear to Salome that John King was not the quiet, kind, gentle man that he had initially appeared to be. Salome bit her bottom lip as she walked towards the house she shared with her mother, remembering the sounds of the arguments she had overheard. John didn't always shout—and yet somehow, in the small, cozy house, his voice raised just enough to put a chill through her. He and Mamm thought she was asleep; but Salome had been wide awake enough to hear him chastising Mamm about every little thing—about putting aside work too soon, or showing too much when she got out of a buggy, or the fact that there was dust on the top of the mantelpiece. Salome shivered.

It seemed to Salome as if John needed to know every detail of everything that happened. When Sarah bought pork or flour in town, John had to know how much she had paid for it, and somehow found something to scold her about. "This food would be better if I knew that you were not wasteful in procuring the ingredients," he had told Salome's mother over dinner one evening. Salome had been too instinctively frightened to say anything in her mother's defense. Normally, she knew, a woman was to be obedient to her man; but John King was not her mother's man, not yet. Sarah had apologized profusely, saying that she had wanted to put a good meal in front of John, knowing that he had worked hard all day.

Another time, John had wanted to know what Sarah had been doing all day when he arrived to take her riding in his buggy. What could have been a reasonable conversation of only a few minutes' duration before changing into a discussion of other things had turned into a lecture of an hour's time that Salome had heard in detail, hidden in the kitchen. "You knew that I would be coming to visit with you, Sarah. You should have gotten more work done. You will be hopelessly behind tomorrow and that will be my fault for indulging you."

"If you do not want to take me riding, John, I am happy to stay at home." Salome had heard a hard, sharp thud—a foreign sound that was becoming more and more familiar to her.

"Nee. If we spend time alone at home too frequently, then everyone will think that we are being inappropriate. We will go riding, because I will not have it said that I am offending your modesty and pushing improper advances or taking liberties with you."

John had also reprimanded her mother over Salome's behavior, telling Sarah, "Your daughter is not yet an adult, you are still responsible for her behavior. I am not your husband yet, but if I am to marry you, I must be sure that she will not bring shame on me." If Salome dallied with her friends running errands, or if she was slow to finish a project her mother assigned her, then John told Sarah that she had to be punished.

He is nothing at all like my father, Salome thought bleakly. Although two years and more after his death, she was starting to lose the sharpness of her memories of her Daed, Salome knew that he would be more understanding than John King was.

None of the other youth in the community seemed to have the kind of strict rules that John King expected her and her mother to live by. Although Salome knew that the private lives of families were their own business, she saw the girls her age dallying—saw them having fun in the warm weather, joking with the boys as they went fishing. If Martha Zook's bonnet came loose on accident, no one accused her of trying to tempt boys to evil thoughts. If Ruth Beiler was late getting back home from running errands, no one seemed to grab her or hover over her threateningly. None of the women she knew seemed to walk in fear of the slightest accident.

It was as though, Salome thought, almost reluctantly climbing the steps up to the front door, John expected everything to be perfect, when the Bible itself said that man was a flawed creature—that the only perfection in the entire world was God Himself. Salome said a silent prayer that John King would find someone else to court instead of her Mamm; the thought of having him as a father was almost unbearable, especially as she came closer and closer to the age of courting herself. If he was acting this sternly before he had even married her Mamm, then what would he be like once he had become the head of the household? She felt a wave of apprehension whenever she considered the question. Salome had heard things about John King; because she was young, she could not be privy to all of the community's gossip, but she had heard whispers that his first wife had died suddenly, and that she had sometimes been seen with strange bruises.

Things were better before, Salome thought—and felt ashamed. If her mother really loved John King, then of course she should marry him. Salome said another prayer to God in her mind, asking that if it was fate that John should marry Sarah, that she and her Mamm would be able to act appropriately enough to avoid a worse fate than the harsh words and scowls of the stern, serious man. Although he had never lifted a hand to hurt her, she had an instinctive feeling that John was somehow capable of it. He insisted that things had to be done his way—not the way that they had always done it.

At first, Salome had bristled at John's ways; she had told her Mamm that occasional accidents were nothing to truly be ashamed of and that while she would take caution not to be immoderate, if her skirt lifted too high or if her bonnet loosened, she would simply correct it and move forward with life. But over time, as Sarah struggled to find a way to live with John, more and more of the man's rules came into Salome's life, and out of fear of exposing her mother to more of John's irritable and angry moods, she had become quieter—at least when she was in any risk of being seen by John. Amongst her friends, Salome could still be herself, but when she was at home, especially if John was visiting, she had to be nearly silent out of respect, and she had to constantly watch herself to make sure she did not spill something—to be accused of wastefulness—or reveal more of her body than was proper, or do anything that John might label as unseemly.

She went into the kitchen where her mother was preparing dinner, forcing a smile on her face. "How was the softball game?" Sarah asked. Salome sat down at the table, taking up a paring knife and a potato to help peel. From the way the ingredients looked, the meal would be wonderful; Salome spotted carrots, late spinach, peas, and corn, and she could smell the unmistakable aroma of a chicken roasting in the wood-fired oven. Under a hand towel, Salome could see the shape of a pie, and the lingering aroma in the air suggested that it was a cherry pie.

"It was a lot of fun! The boys played well." She told her Mamm about Ruth going with her mother to a labor in coming weeks, about some of the other news of her friends that she had gleaned. "David Beiler thinks that he may try playing soccer in the fall, if his work with his Daed will let him."

"He's a born runner," Sarah said with a smile. "An active boy. He'll be a real rowdy when it comes time for his Rumspringa." Salome finished the potatoes, carrying the knife to the sink to wash it, along with her mother's knife.

"Is John King coming for dinner?" she asked, trying to keep her voice as neutral as possible. She didn't want her mother to know how little she liked John, and how afraid of him she was. It was not a lie if she didn't say something that wasn't true.

"I don't think so," Sarah said. "He told me that one of the horses is sick; I think he'll be keeping watch over her all night, to make sure she makes it to the morning." Salome felt a flood of relief; if John wasn't coming over, then things could be normal within the household. "Do you not like John, Salome?" Salome turned to face her mother; she didn't want to lie—she knew that it would be a sin to do so—but the anxiety in her mother's voice made her wish that the truth could be something other than what it was. She took a deep breath. She knew that she had to tell the truth.

"He scares me sometimes, Mamm," Salome said, biting her bottom lip. "He's so stern. He's nothing like Daed." Sarah nodded slowly, her eyes looking sad.

"He's a very particular man, my dear little one," Sarah said, smiling weakly. "I know he sometimes seems difficult and demanding, but it's only because he wants us to be as stable and as steady as possible. And there's nothing wrong with that, is there?" Salome's teeth dug into the soft flesh of her lip as she struggled against saying what would seem disrespectful—even if it was honest. She had to respect that while she dreaded the possibility of a life of John King, her Mamm had the right to determine who she would wed, and if Sarah Lapp wanted to marry John, then Salome would have to learn, somehow, how to live with the stern, cold man.

"I will try to love him better," Salome said finally.

"Try to understand that he is still grieving his wife, and that he has not had an easy life—even before he lost her. His mother was not what she might have been, and he is worried." Salome swallowed down the words that bubbled up from somewhere in the pit of her stomach, taking a deep breath. *If he is still grieving, then it is not a good time for him to be courting!* She knew that it would be disrespectful to say so.

"I will try to understand him better too," she said instead. "But Mamm, he does scare me. I'm afraid—I'm afraid that he might hurt me. Or you." Sarah shook her head.

"He is a good man, a godly man and a minister of our Church," Sarah said, reaching out and pulling Salome in for a quick, tight hug. "He would never do anything to hurt us, I'm certain of it. But we have to give to him a little bit. He will be the head of our home. Pray for understanding." Salome took another breath and nodded.

"I will pray to God," she said. "But I must tell you, Mamm, I'm a little happy he isn't here. I like spending time with you alone." Sarah smiled more brightly.

"Let's get this dinner finished and you can tell me all about everything you heard at the softball game," she suggested, gesturing to the table where the rest of the ingredients for the meal were laid out. "Is your eye on anyone else as much as it is on David Beiler?" Salome's cheeks burned. She had thought that she was being careful, but of course, her mother had noticed the difference.

"My eye isn't on David, he's only a friend." Sarah Lapp grinned, and Salome's blush deepened even as she answered her mother's smile.

"Of course he is only a friend. But you can have very good friends that you want to get to know better." Salome found herself—almost unwillingly at first—telling her mother about David, about talking to him and the funny feeling that rushed through her when they spoke. It felt good to be able to confide in her Mamm, to know that there wouldn't be a scolding for behaving inappropriately, or a lecture on modesty and chastity and obedience. Salome said a silent prayer to God that John King would not be visiting them that night; for she had her mother back, at least for a few hours, and that was well enough of a present.

CHAPTER THIRTEEN

A few weeks later, Salome had put the issue of John King and his observant eyes out of her mind—temporarily at least—as she made her way to a frolic. Now that she was fourteen, only months away from being fifteen, Salome was determined to take every opportunity that she could to enjoy being with her friends in the community. She was almost trembling with excitement as she and her Mamm approached the Fishers' house, where the straw frolic was already beginning to start. Some of the early comers—young men from the community— were already in the hay fields, getting down to work, and Salome couldn't quite resist the urge to seek out David Beiler from amongst the forms either milling around the front yard or out in the fields.

The women would be helping as well as the men; some of the straw would be made into hats both for the Fishers to sell and for the men in the community. Since Salome and her mother were quilters—not hat makers—they would be helping by sorting and cleaning the straw the boys brought in, straw that fell loose from bales or straw that was simply extra. There was not as much urgency to the frolic as there would be to something like a barn raising or shop raising; Salome thought that with the energy the young men brought to the task, they'd have the job done before it was even mealtime, leaving the afternoon for socializing.

Salome followed her mother onto the porch, where the women had gathered; she saw John King with some of the men overseeing the baling and gathering of straw, but he seemed so intent on his task that she couldn't even imagine his stern glance on her. She glanced around once more, and spotted David joking with one of his friends, the two of them playfully tossing straw in each other's direction. She smiled to herself, bowing her head and pretending more devotion to the task of cleaning and straightening the straw she had been given than she felt. Salome felt as if she could nearly burst out of her skin with excitement, and the other girls in the group chattered just as excitedly as she did; even the older women were in great spirits.

The specter of John King didn't weigh on Salome's mind for more than a few minutes as she tried to learn from one of the Fisher girls how to properly plait the straw. Salome was enjoying herself, more than happy to get up and serve the lemonade to the men in the midmorning heat with a few of the other girls, for the chance to get some of her high energy out.

She could never run like David, but she felt as though she wanted to—as if she could understand his quick and fleet feet on the roads that meandered around the community.

The women sang songs that Salome had heard from her earliest memories—songs that were passed down in the Church services, in the evening Sings that the youth all went to. Losing her shyness, Salome added her own voice and found that the work passed even more sweetly, even more quickly, with the aid of a few songs. The men and boys out in the fields, gathering the straw, sang their own songs—almost the same ones—and their voices carried on the light wind, filling the air with sweetness and a kind of fun that Salome wished could go on forever.

When it was time for the meal, Salome went to work with the rest of the girls with an eager will, chipping in wherever she could. Her Mamm had awakened early to make bread rolls to add to the potluck meal, but there were always things to do right before. She helped to load the table that the men would eat at and tried not to obviously look for David as he came back towards the house with the rest of the sweaty, straw-speckled boys, his hat askew on his head, laughing at a joke that Joseph Lapp had told.

She sat down at the table with the women, glancing in the direction of the children's small trestle table. A few years before, she had been relegated to that table, another one of the kinner. It gave her a sense of pride that she was—however junior—one of the women. Salome glanced back at the men's table and saw the boys with them, talking over their food. Her gaze lit on David, seated next to his father, and Salome felt a little jolt of warmth, seeing his smile, his happiness. As she ate, Salome pictured herself in the future, as David's wife; mending his clothes, cooking for him, keeping his house clean. She smiled to herself at the image in her mind. She knew she was young for it yet—but the thought of being a wife, a mother, and especially the wife of David, especially the mother of his children, drew her mind as a flame drew moths.

After lunch, Salome fell into cleaning and clearing with almost as good a will as she had gone into helping prepare the meal. The real work of the day was completed; but since the entire day had been set aside, and it was only two in the afternoon, nobody wanted to go home yet. She knew that once the tables were cleared and the dishes done, the boys would still be out in the yard, and Salome relished the opportunity to spend time with her friends. The boys—their work completely done, with the straw gathered and baled—roughhoused and fooled around, joking and laughing, and the men stood apart in the shade, talking about their various plans for the coming weeks, working up volunteers for a barn raising or discussing a possible fishing expedition if the weather held fine.

Finally, Salome's duties for the frolic were done, and she found herself wandering out into the yard with the other girls, smiling shyly as she spotted David once more. She clung to the knot of girls loitering in the shade of a tree, chatting about the next Sing, and talking about what a nice frolic it had been.

"We're hosting Church next week," Martha Zook said. "Mamm said that she's going to make her special whoopie pies."

"I can bring some of my Mamm's cinnamon bread, too," Miriam Shrock added.

Slowly, as the sense of relaxation grew in the little groups of people, the girls began to move closer to the boys, and the boys closer to the girls. Salome tried not to notice any of the boys in particular, paying most of her attention to her closest friends and the other girls who had come to the frolic. Martha Lapp hadn't been able to come—her mother was too ill to get out of bed, and Martha as the eldest had to stay behind to make sure that the household chores were done; Ruth Beiler was also missing, though Salome heard from one of the other girls that it was because she was behind on her own work, rather than a family trouble.

Salome began to relax, ceasing to even notice who she was speaking to and how close she was to anyone. The boys and girls mingled un-self consciously, joking. Ruth snatched a loose straw out of Joseph's hat, nearly tugging it off of his head, while Miriam ran away from Jacob Yoder, who was trying to shower her with bits of chaff. Salome laughed at something that John Lapp said, and barely noticed that David Beiler was right next to her. "I think we had some of your Mamm's rolls with lunch," David said, and Salome felt her cheeks warming up with a mixture of embarrassment and fascination.

"Mamm got up especially early to make them, I hope you liked them." David smiled back at her shyly.

"They were very good. I hope she's teaching you how to make them." Salome laughed.

"Of course!" She leaned in just a little bit closer to David, unconsciously offering him a conspiratorial smile. "But she told me I won't know all of her secrets until the night before I marry." Her blush deepened still further at the mention of marriage.

Her nerves began to settle as she continued to talk to her friends, her blush subsiding as Salome divided her attention between her girlfriends and the boys of their age group. She was barely aware of the time that passed as she chattered away, smiling and at ease. It felt good to be able to talk to David, to talk to all of her friends. A little bit of leisure time away from work, a little bit of fun, was exactly what she needed.

She was barely aware of the adults close by; Salome knew that her mother would tell her when it was time to go home, but even the men and women seemed to be interested in lingering, enjoying the mild afternoon weather in the shade. She was telling her friends a story about something that had happened to herself and Miriam during the school year— moving around to pantomime the events of the story—and having a great time. Salome heard someone near her gasp, and the boys and girls went completely quiet a mere instant before she felt a shadow falling on her, and then a strong, painful grip on her arm.

John King scowled down at her with a look of impenetrable anger in his eyes. "Come away, Salome," John said harshly, and his grip on her arm tightened as he pulled her away from the cluster of her friends. There was silence all around and Salome's heart beat faster in her chest as the pain in her upper arm intensified. She was so afraid that she couldn't even entertain the idea of resisting him while John King pulled her back towards the buggies that waited for their families. A soft yelp left her lips as tears prickled and stung her eyes. Her father had never done anything like this to her—even if he had felt the need to discipline her, he had avoided grabbing her to do so.

Salome felt utterly hopeless and afraid, and said a silent, panicked prayer in her mind that someone would come to her aid. "John!" The sound of her mother's voice flashed through Salome's mind and her breath left her in a sob of pain and fear. "What are you doing?" Her mother appeared, her face pale and her eyes wide with surprise and a fear that Salome could relate to only too well.

"Your daughter was enticing the boys, Sarah. She was acting immodestly." John's voice came out harsh, as if he could barely hold himself back from shouting. "She must be dealt with immediately and disciplined so that she understands the error of her ways." Salome saw the fear—and the shock— in her mother's eyes. Her mouth was dry, her throat too tight to even enable her to say the slightest word of protest; she had had no idea at all, no notion of trying to entice anyone. *Please, Mamm,* Salome thought, trembling as John's hold on her arm tightened again, sending a new wave of pain through her. She couldn't make herself speak, and for a moment, she was so afraid that her mother would be silent too—that her Mamm, who had always looked out for her, was too frightened to say something to her would-be husband.

Salome saw her mother stand a little straighter, glancing around at the mostly-silent members of the community who were watching everything unfold. "I will take her home and speak with her," Sarah said, her voice trembling. Salome glanced at John, seeing the anger still present in his eyes, the determined set of his lips. What if he grabbed her by the arm, too? She clenched her teeth together, trying to swallow against the tightness she felt in her throat. What would she do?

"I want to be with you," John said lowly. "She needs a father's guidance in this as well as a mother's, before she brings scandal upon herself and shames us all." Salome let of a soft, despairing whimper; she did not know how John intended to discipline her, but some instinct said that it would be much more than just a lecture, much more than shouting. She looked at her mother; Sarah had wilted so many times under John's sternness that for a moment, Salome thought with dread that she would do it again. Instead, her Mamm shook her head, her face taking on firmer lines than Salome had seen in years.

"Nee," she said, her voice unequivocal. "She is my daughter. You are not yet the head of our household, John King. I will speak with her alone." Relief rushed through Salome as John's grip slackened on her arm; as Sarah carefully pulled her away, Salome shook and trembled, tears pouring from her eyes. She glanced back furtively in the direction that they had left John King behind; he was staring at them in abject shock as Sarah helped Salome up into their buggy.

The ride back to their home was silent, with Salome slowly beginning to relax from the rush of panic that had flowed into her body the moment that John's hand had closed around her arm. Salome couldn't believe what had happened to her; she had had an instinctive fear about John for months, but she had never quite been able to entertain the thought that John would actually hurt her.

When they reached their home, Sarah helped Salome to tug the sleeves of her gown down along her arms. Where John had grabbed her, angry bruises had erupted, marring her pale skin, tinged with red on the edges. Sarah swallowed, looking at the sight grimly for a moment. "This might hurt a little bit, bobbel." Salome bit back a cry of pain as Sarah prodded along her arm. "I need to make sure you are not more hurt. I'm sorry, liebchen." After a moment of prodding and feeling, Sarah gave a little nod. "It's just very bad bruising." Salome watched her mother stand and gather up some washing cloths, soft and clean from repeated use and washing.

Sarah dipped the cloths in water she cooled with chips of ice from the icebox, and draped them carefully around Salome's arm. "He was so angry, Mamm," Salome said quietly. "I've never seen anyone so angry in my life."

"I haven't seen him so maddened," Sarah said gravely. She sat down with a sigh. "That should not have happened." Sarah shook her head and Salome looked down at her arm.

"I promise, Mamm. I wasn't trying to entice the boys. I was just telling a story—to everyone, the boys and the other girls." Salome's eyes stung as her tears started again. "I wasn't even thinking about trying to entice anyone!" Sarah nodded, rising to hug her for a moment. Salome's mother smoothed her tears away, stepping to the pantry to take out some sweet rolls she had made the morning before.

"Here, bobbel," Sarah said with a tired smile. "We'll change the cloths in a few minutes and get the bruises down on you."

"I'm afraid of him, Mamm," Salome admitted. "He could become angry like that again, towards you instead of with me." Sarah closed her eyes.

"I will pray on it, Salome. I…" she shook her head, opening her eyes and holding Salome's gaze. "I am in no hurry, and I will need to be convinced that John will master his temper before I will ever consent to marry him." There was a brittle note of anger in her mother's voice; unlike John's anger, her mother's indignation comforted Salome. She ate her sweet roll slowly and didn't flinch when her mother changed the cool cloths on her arm.

Some time later there was a knock at the door. Salome felt a frisson of fear. "Stay here, liebchen." Salome nodded, trying to relax. Sarah stood and walked to the front door of the house.

Salome's heart was beating faster in her chest as she heard her mother open the door. "John," Sarah said, sounding uneasy.

"Where is Salome?" Salome shivered at the sound of John's voice. She thought to herself that she would never again be able to hear John's voice without fear.

"She's inside," Sarah said, her voice gaining slightly in confidence.

"I will speak with her. She needs to be disciplined, and I know you have not done it."

"Nee, you will not. You will leave, John King." Salome heard a thudding sound and gasped, a twinge of sympathetic pain echoing through her bruised arm.

"She should not have been with a mixed group, Sarah. She is already turning wayward and you are doing nothing to check her!" Salome put her hands over her ears, trembling as the shouting increased.

CHAPTER FOURTEEN

When he saw John King grab young Salome Lapp by the arm, pulling her away from the group of youths she was speaking with, Mark Shrock felt the same shock that went through everyone attending the straw frolic. For a moment, stunned, he simply watched as his fellow minister led the young woman away, dragging her towards the buggies as her tears began to fall in fear and pain.

But when the girl's mother, Sarah, went towards the two, intervening on her daughter's behalf—the way that a good mother should, Mark thought—the action shook him out of his sense of dismayed surprise. Mark watched with a certain humble pride as Sarah extracted her daughter from John's angry grip, bringing her away. For a long moment, John watched the two women leave, stunned—obviously—that Sarah had had the courage to stand up to him. Mark smiled to himself, thinking that Sarah had demonstrated the best virtues associated with the women of the bible in her actions to protect her daughter.

After a few moments, John's surprise left him, and Mark watched as the angry man stormed towards his buggy; fearing for whoever John might encounter, and telling himself that he had only a normal concern for the Lapps, two women alone in their home, Mark moved towards his own buggy as John drove away from the frolic. The peace of the social event had been utterly disrupted, but Mark thought that it would find itself again soon enough with the disturbance well away; he just hoped that John would not be foolish enough to harm himself or someone else in the depths of his anger.

Mark had seen John angry like this a few times; never quite as bitterly enraged as this, but Mark knew his minister enough to know that John had never made substantial progress in controlling an unruly temper. The thought of that rage directed at Sarah Lapp—who Mark knew was tentatively courting the other man—filled Mark with a kind of anxious dread. Sarah, of all the women in the community, should not be the object of such anger. Mark corrected himself; no one should be the object of such wrath. *I am not concerned because it is Sarah. I am concerned because John is in a wrathful state of mind.* Mark shied away from thoughts of the need to protect Sarah in particular; she was courting a man—he could not interfere with that courtship.

Mark followed John through the lanes until the other man reached the Lapp home, leaping from his buggy. It was obvious to Mark that John was just as full of rage as he had been the moment he had left the frolic; Mark hung back, saying a silent prayer in his mind that God would give him the right judgment in how to handle the situation. He watched—telling himself that it was Sarah's place to decide whether or not John could come in—as the other man knocked at the Lapps' door hard. Mark watched grimly as Sarah appeared at the door, looking frightened but determined.

He heard John's accusation—that Salome had been deliberately enticing the young men at the frolic—and Mark frowned. He had paid little attention to the youths, but that was because he hadn't noticed anything untoward. Salome Lapp was a godly young woman, and Mark had taken an interest in her, from an appropriate distance, from the time that Sarah's husband had passed away two years before. He wanted to make sure that Salome was doing well in the wake of her Daed's passing, and it seemed to him that her grief had proceeded normally.

As the argument between John and Sarah became heated, Mark felt his anger at his fellow minister beginning to well up. Sarah told John quite clearly to leave her home, that she would not permit him inside; as she struggled to get the door closed, Mark saw that John had put his booted foot in the way, blocking the door. He shook his head; John was not only showing an inappropriate, sinful amount of anger—he was now outraging the modesty of a woman.

Mark leaped down from his buggy, walking quickly to the porch where John and Sarah struggled. "John King," Mark said, lifting his voice enough to be heard over the other two. John started, turning to look in Mark's direction. "It's time to leave, John. Sarah has barred you from her home."

"I am courting her," John said savagely. "She cannot make me leave so easily, and neither can you." Mark looked at Sarah's scared face and shook his head sadly.

"John, if you do not do the right thing and go home right now, I will speak with the Bishop about your misdeeds." He held John's gaze steadily. "You have let your anger run away with you, and it is time to excuse yourself." At the mention of the Bishop, John's face blanched. He looked—for a moment— as though he would persist; but the next minute, John reluctantly withdrew his foot, turning away abruptly and walking with a stiff-legged gait back to his buggy.

Mark watched as John left in sullen silence, his face like stone. He carefully approached Sarah, who sagged against the doorframe, trembling slightly. Mark wished that there were something more that he could offer the scared woman other than his sympathy and understanding. "Are you all right, Sarah?" he asked quietly. Sarah gathered herself, taking a breath, and Mark admired the woman's courage.

"I think so," Sarah said, turning her big, dark eyes up to look at him. Mark smiled softly; his hand itched to smooth the loose lock of her blonde hair back underneath Sarah's bonnet—but that would be unseemly. Instead he turned his attention onto the real matter at hand.

"How is Salome?" Sarah glanced over her shoulder into the house.

"He bruised her arm," Sarah said quietly, dropping her voice lowly enough that even her daughter within would not hear it. "I'm scared, Mark. He frightens me greatly when he's like this." Mark nodded.

He thought of the rumors he had heard about John King; murmurs about the way the man had treated his first wife. When he had heard through community gossip that John was courting with Sarah Lapp, he had been deeply concerned. But it was none of his business. "I can only recommend that you take the matter to God. But if you are afraid of him, perhaps you should slow your courting down." Sarah hesitated before nodding.

"I am no longer certain I want to marry him at all," Sarah said, shaking her head. "I...I know that I should have a husband, and Salome needs a father, but I do not know that John is the right person." Mark remembered the sight of John's first wife—the way she had appeared at Church one time, the right side of her face marred by a bruise that the woman had anxiously said she'd received taking a tumble into a wood bin the day before. He had had misgivings about John King and about the nature of the man as a husband from that day, never quite trusting the story.

"Please tell me if there is anything that I can do to help you, Sarah," Mark said, unable to quite keep himself from saying what he really wanted to—but unwilling to say more when he knew that Sarah had not told John outright to call off the courtship.

"I will. Thank you, Mark," Sarah said, smiling. "I should get back to Salome." Mark nodded. He held her gaze for a moment longer before turning away reluctantly, walking back to his buggy. He glanced over his shoulder and saw Sarah going back into her home. For reasons that Mark could not bring himself to examine in detail, he felt strangely sad as he jumped back up into the front of his buggy as Sarah disappeared behind her door. She was safe from John's rage; that was the important thing. Mark told himself that he would look into the matter of John King's temper in more detail—it was concerning to see a minister of the community behaving in the way he had, especially with the murmurs that had gone around about John's first wife's sudden death. Mark put any thought of Sarah Lapp in particular out of his mind and drove back to the frolic, hoping that his nerves and agitation would settle.

CHAPTER FIFTEEN

Although he had prayed on the issue several times, David found himself unable to quite forget his strange encounter with the Englischer running coach. It had been months since he had encountered the man on the byways of Bird-in-Hand, but while David was certain he couldn't bring himself to violate the Ordnung, he couldn't help but wonder what it would be like to have been born to a different life; to be born an Englisch boy instead of Amish. He knew the thought was presumptuous—it possibly even questioned the will of God himself—but David couldn't help thinking about it.

David forced himself to focus on the things that he knew; he loved the work with his Daed, and he knew that if he violated the Ordnung, he would bring troubles upon his Mamm. He knew that even though he was too young to think of courting, he cared more about Salome Lapp than any other girl he had met before. These were all important things; and

David was able to put aside his vain dreams in the hope of something better, more substantial, and more real.

He was relieved that he had refused the Englischer coach's offer, but as his responsibilities at the carpentry increased, there were fewer opportunities for David to run. His father watched him more closely, and David knew that it was right that Black David should do so, but he yearned for more opportunities to let his feet pick up their pace, to let them carry him with the wind rushing past his ears. There was something so sweetly like freedom in the long and winding paths around the community, something that David craved. *If I could join the Englisch running team, I could feel that way more often.* But not only would joining the team require him to continue his education beyond what the Ordnung said was correct; it would also mean competing, seeking glory for himself, another violation of the community's laws. David knew that since he had not yet decided to join the Church, he would not be banished from the community for it; and he had heard of many young men doing similar things during their Rumspringa. But he could still bring scandal upon his family, especially if he chose to explore that possibility before he could take his Rumspringa.

David took all of the opportunities that he could to let his legs wind out underneath him, running to and from the shop and home, running on his errands for his Daed, running to make his visits to friends' homes. But there was something more that he craved that David could not quite find words to express. He had spoken about it to his father, as well as he could understand it. Working in the carpentry shop, David found many opportunities for speaking with Black David, chances that he could not have at home. He did not want to alarm his Mamm.

"Daed," David had said, as he worked at sanding the rough sides of a set of cabinets, "I don't understand it. I'm happy with my life, but somehow I also want more." Black David had given him a slight smile.

"You're coming into your restless years," Black David had told him. "Your years of schooling are done, and you're eager for the next part of your life. It's a good thing, but don't let your whims pull you around." Black David had gone on to explain that this was a time in men's lives when they were challenged and tested by God; they had to learn to make their own choices and decisions, and that could only come with making the occasional mistake, and with making decisions and seeing what the consequences of those choices were.

The explanation had comforted David temporarily; he thought that his craving for something more—his desire, sinful though he knew it to be, to taste freedom in the form of competition amongst Englischers—was something that would pass away with time, going away as he made more decisions in his life, as he came closer to being an adult. But in spite of feeling more satisfaction than ever with his work, and more interest in staying near so that he could court Salome when the time came for them to consider their lives as adults in the community, David couldn't help but occasionally remember the encounter with the coach and wonder how it would have been if the Ordnung had been different, if there had been a chance for him to take the opportunity the coach had presented without turning his back on the community.

David's thoughts were on the subject as he trailed behind his Daed and Mamm, following them into the town. As he had taken on more responsibilities in the carpentry shop, David had also taken on more chores at home, and Black David and Barbara Beiler had both agreed—though David was not aware of it—that increasing their son's at-home responsibilities would also help him through the difficult years of transition. So they both made excuses for needing his help in bringing home purchases from the town, or needing his help at home, whenever David was not either working at the shop or socializing with his friends.

David kept to a respectful distance from his parents as his Daed walked through the small hardware store that Bird-in-Hand boasted. Although Black David took very good care of all of his tools, there was inevitably wear and tear, and sometimes things could no longer be repaired and had to be replaced; in addition, Daed said that it was time for David to have tools of his own to use. "We will buy you a new item each week, so that you can build up your proper collection gradually," Black David had said when the plan had begun.

They had taken the buggy into town, and David halfway wished that he could have followed his parents at a run instead of riding along with them; but there would be heavy things—such as a barrel of flour for his mother's baking—that couldn't be run with. David listened to the hum of conversation around him; the Bird-in-Hand community wasn't restricted, or constrained behind fences of any kind, and Englischer men and women and children interacted with the Amish community. David had long sense ceased to be embarrassed or even irritated by the questions that Englischers posed.

It was as he was following his parents through the general store, listening to them discuss the merits of various purchases, that David felt the gaze on him; the feeling wasn't like being stared at by tourists or regular Englisch people—his hair stood up on the back of his neck. It felt the same way it did when he had been younger, playing hide-and-seek with some of the other boys in the community, and the seeker had spotted him. David looked around, and saw the very Englischer running coach he had been thinking of. A feeling of something like guilt washed through him; it was impossible for a moment not to entertain the thought that his own selfish thoughts had drawn the man somehow, that God was bringing this choice to test his resolve to live right once more.

The coach—David remembered that his name was Rod Travis—was unquestionably looking at him. "Mamm, Daed," David said quietly, drawing their attention. He hoped that there would be no confrontation; but the hope began to evaporate as the coach began to approach.

The Englischer held up his hands as a gesture of peace as he walked towards them, and David glanced at his parents, uncertain of what to do. "I won't repeat my offer," the coach said, as soon as he was within speaking distance. "I just want to speak peacefully with you." David glanced at his parents; Black David nodded slightly.

"We will hear you through," Black David said. The coach turned his attention onto David more fully.

"When did you become interested in running, son?" David shrugged.

"It's always been something I loved," David said. "I never thought of it as something to be proud of—my Daed says haste makes waste, and our teachings are that a slower way of life is better." The coach nodded slowly.

"You are a natural, David. I hope that your father has a good use for your ability." He glanced at Black David and smiled. "A boy with your inclination must be more than a little rambunctious." David saw his Mamm smile slightly, suppressing a greater expression of amusement with an effort. "I just want to know why it is that you're not able to join the team." David glanced at his parents again; if they wanted to explain to this Englischer about the Ordnung, it was not his place—particularly as an unbaptized member of the church— to do it instead. His father rested a hand on his shoulder, moving forward slightly.

"He cannot continue schooling, it is against the rules of our church," Black David said in a level tone. "He's reached the end of what we consider to be appropriate education, and he's starting to learn about his future trade."

"What trade is he going into?" the coach asked, and David realized that Rod was genuinely curious, and genuinely interested.

"He will be a carpenter, as I am," Black David said. "Now that he has reached the age of fifteen, his responsibilities are growing. He is needed more around the shop, and at home, since he will soon be a man."

"That's a weighty responsibility indeed," the coach said, nodding in understanding. "I don't know very much about your culture—I hope you don't mind my questions." Black David shook his head.

"We do not mind honest curiosity." The coach smiled.

"So he can't continue school—but there are other ways that he could compete, that he could become a runner. I would be happy to train him; it wouldn't take any time away from his apprenticeship." Black David shook his head.

"Our Ordnung—our orders and rules for living—forbid us from putting ourselves into a position to seek individual glory." The coach frowned in thought, and David wondered if there would be a debate—if the Englischer coach would try to convince his Daed that he should, indeed, try and seek glory.

"Is it something like the sin of pride, in the bible?" Black David nodded.

"It is very much like that. Pride is one of the worst sins that a man can commit; by seeking to indulge pride, we lead ourselves into deeper and more desperate sins, ones that cannot be as easily remedied." The coach considered this, and David could see that he was taking his Daed's words seriously, that he wasn't just dismissing the ideas as "quaint" or "backwards" as he had heard so many Englischers call the Amish.

"I remember a verse—I am probably not as knowledgeable as someone who I assume spends much more time reading the bible—but I remember reading a verse that said, 'Humble yourselves in the presence of God, and He will exalt you.' Is that something like what you seek?" Black David nodded; so did David's Mamm, and David found himself nodding too— although the wording was not precisely as he himself remembered it.

"That is right, and it is very important to our community and our Church to strive to be humble in all things." The coach nodded again. He extended his hand.

"I want to ask your forgiveness. I made my offer in ignorance, and I want you to know that I respect your beliefs and will not try and push you to violate them." David watched as his Daed took the man's hand and shook it firmly. "Will you forgive me too, David?" The coach extended his hand to him, and David shook it firmly, glancing at his parents for confirmation.

Finally, the coach turned his attention onto Barbara Beiler. "I hope that you'll forgive me too, ma'am," the Englischer said. "I shouldn't have frightened and alarmed you the way I did, and I an deeply sorry that I invaded your privacy." David saw his mother hesitate; he knew that she was deeply concerned about whether or not he would stay within the community. After his mother's sister had left the community, banished by the Meidung, it had weighed on Mamm's mind that David might be tempted out of the right way. "I promise you—I will never trouble you with an offer that violates the rules of your community again." After only a moment longer, Barbara extended her hand, and shook the coach's hand.

"I forgive you," Barbara said, smiling. "I am very glad that you understand we want what we believe is best for our children."

"I understand completely," the coach said. "I hope you won't mind it if I sometimes admire your son's talent; I will never bother him about it—but as a coach in the skill that he's so good at, I appreciate watching his innate ability." Black David hesitated, and David wondered if there might be something he didn't understand, some rule against what the coach had proposed.

"As long as you do understand that my son cannot join your school or your team, I do not see that it would do any harm." Black David glanced at him, and David nodded.

"I appreciate you speaking to me. Have a blessed day." As the coach left them, David smiled to himself. He was glad that the conversation had gone so well, that there was no confrontation and no need for angry words. It was good of the coach to have attempted to understand—though he knew that the Englischer couldn't ever fully comprehend why the Ordnung was so important. But he was contented, and it seemed as though his prayers to God, for some kind of answer to the craving he felt and the curiosity he couldn't talk himself out of, had been answered.

CHAPTER SIXTEEN

Rod Travis was disappointed that he wouldn't be able to prevail upon David Beiler or his parents to get the boy to join the team and continue schooling; young David was such a natural runner that it seemed a shame for the boy's talent to go to waste. But after his conversation with the Beiler family—begun on an impulse when he spotted them in the town general store—he could understand that their religion, while foreign to him, had reasons for the requirements it made on its followers. He began to read up on the Amish of the county, learning about their way of life, and respected the fact that they had managed to successfully hold themselves apart from the world—while still managing to have some awareness of what went on in it.

The running coach in Rod could not quite resist the need to occasionally check up on David as the summer gave him more time to himself; since Bird-in-Hand didn't have fences or any other physical barriers separating the Amish community from the more modern residents, so Rod thought that as long as he didn't stalk the boy, appreciating his skill as a runner from a distance would not be untoward. Rod caught sight of David around the town, running with parcels in his hands for his father, or last-minute needs for his mother. A few times, Rod had the opportunity to talk to David himself; the teen was candid and open—and Rod knew better than to approach the topic of track and cross country, or even continued education.

They encountered each other at the general store, or at the town hardware store, and Rod asked after David's parents, about his progress as a carpentry apprentice. "Seems like I see you running everywhere you go," Rod jokingly commented to the boy, resisting the urge to reach over and tousle David's dark hair the way he would one of his track team members. David laughed.

"I really do prefer running," David admitted. "Unless the weather is very poor, or I have to carry something heavy or sharp, I always run wherever I go. It's better even than taking the buggy." Rod found himself grinning.

"How much do you think you run in a day?" Rod watched as David did the math in his mind; as a future carpenter, Rod thought, David would have need of good math skills—at least geometry. David shrugged.

"Maybe about ten or twelve miles? I don't always keep count, since I'm running so often." Rod shook his head in amazement. The boy ran easily ten or twelve miles a day, and looked as though he was running perhaps one or two. He would be a match, Rod thought, for the prowess of the Masaai of Africa at that kind of endurance and speed.

Usually, Rod tried to avoid speaking too much with David; he wasn't concerned with getting the boy to change his mind—or with the fallout for himself and for David if he did—but he knew that now the reasons had been made clear to him, he should avoid trying to become too close to the family without their invitation. But he was content to watch David run around the community, taking an athletically minded pleasure in David's form, his economy of movement, his pacing.

Rod was beginning to learn more and more about the community that he had moved to; he was learning about the ways of the Amish, and while he wished that he could prevail upon David to explore the possibilities open to an athlete of his talents during his Rumspringa, he knew that it was not his place to tempt someone from their chosen path. He had to admire from afar, because he knew that if he let himself speak to David too often, his earnest wish to convince the boy to use his talents for something less mundane than getting around the tight-knit community more quickly would come through in time.

One day, as he was watching David from a seat outside of one of the shops in the town center, a movement in his peripheral vision interrupted Rod's thoughts. "You're watching David Beiler run?" someone said; Rod turned to see one of his fellow teachers, Angela Meadows.

"He's a good runner," Rod said, continuing to watch the teen. "I enjoy watching him—great form, great pacing, no wasted effort." He shook his head in amazement as the boy turned a corner, taking him out of sight.

"Rod, I know you want him on your team," Angela said, giving him a wry grin. "If I were a track coach I'd probably offer him however much money I possibly could to get him into high school. But he's following a different path." Rod held up his hands, gesturing that he understood.

"I asked him a while back, before I knew better; I haven't asked him since. He's a great runner, and if he were one of us—what do they call us, Englischers? If he were a non-Amish kid, I'd do whatever I could to persuade him. But I understand. He's got a different life planned for himself, and different rules to follow. I just like to watch him." Angela smiled again.

"I've taught lots of Amish kids in my classes for years now—it still makes me a little sad to know that once they leave my class, they won't be going on to learn more." Angela glanced at a group of Amish girls, walking together through the town with baskets of purchases for their mothers. "But they must have something going on—something they're doing right. Even with the Rumspringa, the majority of the youths decide to join the church." Angela shrugged and looked at Rod. "I'm glad you understand." Rod exhaled, relieved that he wasn't going to get a scolding from Angela.

"I wish it could be different, but I have to respect someone's beliefs." Angela nodded again, and gave Rod a little wry smile.

"Until I remembered you coached boys' track and cross-country, for a second there I thought you were peeping at the poor kid." Rod sputtered.

"No! No—no, no, no." Angela laughed.

"I realized that as someone who trains people to run better, you were probably just impressed with a natural talent. Now if you were watching the young Amish girls…" Angela tilted her head to the side. "Relax, Rod. I don't think you're some pervert. Maybe don't be so obvious about staring in the future so people who don't know you so well don't get the wrong idea." Rod sighed, shaking his head. He had to admit—from the outside—that it would probably be suspicious. He'd be more careful in the future not to come across as some creep.

CHAPTER SEVENTEEN

In the wake of the straw frolic, when John King had attacked Salome, David Beiler found himself feeling real fear for the girl he saw as a friend—and potentially, in the future, as more than that. He knew the whispers about John around the community; whispers that had increased after the assault. While he hadn't seen the bruises on Salome's arm for himself, the common knowledge of all of the people of the community was that the girl had been injured, and that Sarah Lapp had barred him from her home.

When David heard of it from one of Salome's cousins, he had felt anger at first—anger that a man who was a minister in the community, who should be the best of everything that David had been taught to hold dear, had resorted to violence in a fit of temper. Christ himself had said, and David had grown up knowing as truth, that violence was never the answer, and that even when provoked, it was better to turn the other cheek rather than to offer harm to another person. And Salome herself had done nothing—she had not threatened or hurt John King in any way, and had not even been guilty of anything other than having fun with the other youths at the frolic; exactly the purpose of the social event.

But concern for Salome's safety began almost immediately to replace his frustration and anger. David knew that there was not very much—presently—that the community could do about John King. Sarah Lapp had not formally broken off the courtship with the man, so until something changed, Salome would have to be irreproachable in John's eyes. David was determined not to give John King any reason to attack Salome again; the idea of something worse happening to the girl he felt so strongly for made David's stomach turn over. He prayed that Salome would be able to keep safe, among the other prayers that filled his mind throughout the day.

Taking a practical approach, David insisted to Salome when they ran into each other, running errands for their parents, that they would have to take care. "I enjoy speaking to you, but I don't want for John King to get angry with you again," David told her gently. "So from now on, I won't speak to you unless we're in a group." Salome's eyes still had a soft glow of fear in them as she nodded, accepting what David said.

"But I was in a group when he grabbed me," she told him quietly. "I wasn't marking anyone out. You're my friend, David—I should be able to talk to you like I can anyone." David frowned, wishing that he could offer a different solution;

but the only ones who could say or do anything about John King were the members of the church themselves. All he could do, David knew, was to try and help to keep Salome out of John's range of temper.

It disappointed him that they could no longer meet each other in the streets and paths, and enjoy each other's company to while away the travels. For Salome, David would even slow down his run, walk instead of hurrying from one place to another; but no longer. He would have to make sure that he didn't show any remarkable signs of regard for the girl—that John King couldn't say that Salome was enticing him, or that he was making untoward advances.

In the wake of the incident, David thought of all of the other times that he had encountered John King dealing with and talking to Salome; it was no secret to him—or, it seemed, to the community as a whole—that John King seemed to want to control both Lapp women. But though there were rumors of shouting fights and arguments, and Salome and Sarah had both become quieter, more fearful versions of themselves, until the incident at the straw frolic, no one had worried overmuch. David had overheard some of the adults of the community saying that these were the kinds of things that could happen when two adults, set in their ways, tried to come to an agreement about how their lives together would be.

But no one could completely ignore what John had done to Sarah. Murmurs went around the community about John King's first wife and her sudden passing, about how strange it was that a woman who had been perfectly healthy could fall so quickly ill and die. Some were saying that the community as a whole should take action about John King, or that the Bishop should be spoken to; but as yet, nothing had happened, and David found himself fearful for Salome and her mother alike.

A few weeks after the incident, as the concern in the Bird-in-Hand community began to fade, David was running to a volleyball game, thinking of Salome. He wished that they could have one of their one-on-one conversations again; but he had been careful not only to avoid being alone with her, but to also make sure that he put himself on the opposing team to Salome whenever he played either volleyball or softball with her. The upcoming game was a social event for the whole community; instead of a pickup game, the adults would be watching. There were not as many tasks around the various farms that needed to be done in the midsummer, and sports were more popular than at any other time of the year.

David arrived at the volleyball courts, smiling at his friends who had come out earlier. Salome was with the girls, talking and laughing, and David made himself look away from her after just a momentary glance. Looking around the clearing surrounding the court, David also saw Sarah Lapp, as well as John King. They were not speaking to each other, but Sarah was not making any moves to get away from the man. David wondered with amazement that Sarah could actually endure being around a man like John King; it made no sense.

The two teams took up their positions on the opposite sides of the net and David caught Salome's eye for just an instant, giving her a quick smile of reassurance. He preferred to be on her team—before things had become so intolerable with John King, David had done whatever he could to end up on the same team as Salome, because they played well together, and because he liked the opportunity to speak with her. But there was not much lost in being on the opposing team; he could still watch her play, interact with her, and he wasn't putting her at risk of inciting John's wrath.

The game started easily, with both sides taking their positions and moving around easily. David watched Salome's play, and occasionally smiled at her, though he forced himself to pay more attention to his own team. Salome's team scored a point as one of the girls on David's team, Martha Zook, barely missed the ball; then David's team scored, thanks to a powerful hit from John Fisher. Back and forth the game ebbed and flowed, and David found himself more and more absorbed in the play itself—not thinking about John King's presence, or the fact that he had to be cautious about interacting with Salome. He and the other members of both teams were laughing and enjoying themselves, and a relaxed, social atmosphere filled the air.

On Salome's team, Samuel King botched a serve; both teams rushed the net as the ball came down, and David found himself rushing right along with the rest of the players on his side. As he launched himself towards the net to try and make a grab for the ball, he found himself—to his instant chagrin—bumping into Salome. He caught the instant flash of fear in Salome's eyes, and felt his heart beating faster as he realized what had happened—and remembered that John King was watching. He was shocked, but not surprised, when he heard John King's voice, rising above the hum of the two teams and the adults and younger kids watching the game. "Salome!" The sound of brittle rage sent a torrent of cold fear through David's body.

CHAPTER EIGHTEEN

Mark Schrock had felt a flicker of concern when he saw that John King was attending the volleyball game that the youths were playing; but he told himself that there was nothing that even John King could be capable of misconstruing as an attempt on Salome's part to entice the young men of the community. It was a simple game, with mixed teams on both sides; the girls playing had all been careful to ensure that there would be no immodesties, as they always were.

In the wake of the incident at the straw frolic, Mark had found himself more and more concerned about the nature of John King's attention and focus on Sarah and Salome Lapp. The fact that Sarah had not broken off the courtship completely, making her wish to remain single known, made Mark feel uneasy for the widow; he knew that she might consider herself less-than-preferred in finding a new husband, but to his mind—though he forced himself to avoid thinking about it when the thoughts came up—there was no woman in the community who was better suited to being a wife and mother than Sarah. When Sarah had become widowed by the passing of her husband, Mark—whose wife had passed away before—briefly turned his thoughts onto the subject of potentially courting her.

But he had let himself be guided by the Ordnung, and he had avoided making any advances, waiting patiently for the time when it would be appropriate to approach her. When he had discovered that John King, his fellow minister, had approached Sarah, and she had accepted his advances, Mark had told himself that he would have to forget about her completely; unless Sarah decided to reject John King, he had no right to set himself up as competition for her favor and love.

Mark allowed himself to relax as the game progressed, speaking to the other parents and community adults who had come to watch. He glanced every so often at where Sarah Lapp and John King stood—together, a few feet of distance between them, but a slightly chilled air belying any thought that the two were fully reconciled. Sarah herself looked apprehensive; not quite frightened, but on edge. It was a look in her eyes, on her face, that made Mark feel frustrated almost to the point of anger. Their way was to be nonviolent, to turn the other cheek. The Ordnung was clear that violence was sinful, and that rage—the lack of control over one's temper—was a major character flaw that should be mindfully and carefully prayed on and disciplined. As a minister, John had an even greater responsibility to see to his faults; after all, Mark thought, Christ himself had been very clear. "And why beholdest thou the mote that is in thy brother's eye, but considerest not the beam that is in thine own eye? Or how wilt thou say to thy brother, Let me pull out the mote out of thine eye; and, behold, a beam is in thine own eye? Thou hypocrite, first cast out the beam out of thine own eye; and then shalt thou see clearly to cast out the mote out of thy brother's eye," the Gospel of Matthew had quoted Christ as saying. If John King set himself up as an advisor and monitor of the community's spiritual well being, then he was even more responsible for attending to his own faults.

Mark told himself that his concern was truly—and only— that John King as a minister should be held responsible for his faults, and that he would be just as concerned with any of the members of the Bird-in-Hand community who were exposed to the minister's wrath. He prayed on the issue, and asked for God to show him what he should do: to protect two vulnerable women in his community, to advise Sarah if she came to him, and to resolve the situation if it came to it. He had come close on several occasions to addressing the issue of John King with Bishop Fisher, but somehow Mark told himself that as long as it was not brought directly to him, he couldn't intervene.

Mark knew that he was not the only person in the community who had noticed what had passed between John, Sarah, and Salome. While Sarah had not come to ask for his intervention, a few of the members of the community, concerned about what they had seen, had mentioned it to him on various occasions in the weeks since the straw frolic. Mark had held himself back from saying anything that could be considered malicious gossip or bearing false witness, but the murmurs in the community about the strangeness of John King's first wife's death had increased for a short time, and he could not bring himself to quite scold the people who repeated the rumors.

Mark had never known John King very well; even before John had become a minister in the Church, he had been a quiet and self-contained man. Losing his first wife had rendered the man into a near-hermit in his grief. John continued to attend to his duties as a minister, and he had made trips to sell the surplus vegetables and dairy from his farm, but he was not prone to visiting, and rarely came to frolics. Mark knew that John had been a quiet boy as well. Part of the reason why John had been elected as a minister for the community was that he was so quiet, and seemed to be so patient and gentle.

Mark recalled that very little was known, overall, about John King's first wife. She had been a member of the community, had gone to school with the other youth her age, but had always been somewhat meek. The wedding had been a quiet affair, and after that, Ruth had seemed to all but disappear; the few times she was seen in public, she was even quieter than usual, but protested that the only reason that she did not go out amongst the community very often was that she was very busy around the home, helping John with the farm. More than once, she had turned visitors away, saying that she or John were ill, and a few of those occasions, Mark recalled, some of the members of the community had remarked that she had had a strange bruise here or there, which she always explained away by saying that she had been clumsy.

When Ruth had passed away so suddenly, John had explained to his neighbors that she had always been unwell; Mark remembered that there was some suggestion that her death might have been to do with problems in a pregnancy, but of course the Kings were so quiet in the community, and no one could have asked Ruth herself about being pregnant. It eventually lapsed into the kind of rumor that people tended to ignore; since there was no way to get to the bottom of it, everyone assumed that a man who was a minister could not have done something so terrible as to kill his own wife. Mark himself had thought it impossible.

But now that the more controlling aspects of John King's behavior were coming to light, everyone was whispering again. Mark was proud of the fact that he lived in a very sociable community, where neighbors helped each other and bonds were as tightly knit as they could possibly be; at the end of the day, everyone was at least distantly related to everyone else, though care was taken that two very close relatives not come together in matrimony. Nothing was entirely secret in their community, however, and people were beginning to talk about what a shame it was that Sarah Lapp was having such a difficult time with her courting, and it was a shame that John King had made his move first. That there were other, equally deserving men who would make a good husband for her.

Mark had also noticed the ways in which Salome and Sarah had both isolated themselves. Salome tended more than ever to stay near to the home, and when she ran errands with her mother, they moved with an unaccustomed quickness, rarely lingering to speak to anyone. Salome had an apprehensive look to her, and she kept a distance from all of the young men of the community, doing everything she could to speak only with other girls. But not mingling with all of the youths of her age was strange for an Amish girl; none of the other girls of her age were so distant from the boys, even occasionally avoiding mixed groups. Some of the girls were in far more danger of immodesty than Salome was.

Mark watched the game, thinking of young David Beiler. He had been pleased when Black David had mentioned that he, his wife, and his son had spoken with the Englischer coach and explained about the Ordnung, and about their way of life. Mark had heard nothing about the matter of the running coach since that time, though he had seen the man watching David run. It was harmless enough, as long as the Englisch did not attempt to lead the boy astray.

Privately, Mark thought that young David had plenty of reasons to want to stay in the community; though of course at fifteen and fourteen, the two teens could not make any outward show of preference, Mark was astute enough to notice the way that David took care with Salome, keeping himself carefully distant from her. Even if it was no more than a deep friendship, David clearly cared about and for the girl. If both youths were able to make it through the age of high spirits and decided after their Rumspringa to join the church, Mark was fairly certain that they would eventually wed, though that was years in the future for both of them.

Mark's nervousness began to settle as the game went on, and eventually he let himself believe that there would not possibly be a recurrence of the event at the straw frolic. John King had taken the warning that Mark had given him, and he was apparently attending to his behavior, though Mark would have been more relieved to hear that Sarah had barred him from her and her daughter's life completely. He watched as the game ebbed and flowed, one team scoring a point and then the other team countering. While the community's Ordnung did not allow for individuals to seek glory in any way—considering it a form of pride—team sports were very popular, and the two teams teased each other playfully as they continued in the game, taunting each other good-naturedly as they played.

When a serve came close to the net—close enough for both teams to launch themselves at it, to be the ones to get it over and onto the other side—Mark felt a flicker of tension lance through him. The moment that David and Salome collided, barely bumping each other, he knew that something would go wrong; on cue, as if his own negative thoughts had conjured the bad event, he heard John King shouting Salome's name. Just as clearly, Mark saw Salome's head turn towards the man, saw her face blanch and her eyes widen in fear. He knew, in that moment, that John King had done absolutely nothing to mend his ways; he had merely made his controlling and harmful, temperamental actions harder for the community to see. Mark looked around, spotting Bishop Fisher.

As John King made his way towards Salome Lapp from his position on the sidelines, Mark got the Bishop's attention quickly. The older man had reacted to the tone of John King's voice just as much as anyone in the gathering, and the minute Mark called his name, the Bishop's gaze connected with his and he nodded. Mark and Bishop Fisher moved quickly, cutting across the grass to intercept John King, who was stalking towards Salome with intent and anger as plain as day in his eyes.

"John King," the Bishop said, pitching his voice to be heard readily over the murmurs of dismay and disturbance that filled the air. "We need to speak." John staggered to a stop and Mark approached with the Bishop at his side; he took one of John's arms, though not as harshly as John had taken Salome's weeks before, while the Bishop took the other, and between the two men they steered John towards an open barn near the volleyball court.

John King protested, squirming in Mark's grip, but he would not—Mark knew—make any of the kind of moves that he would try with a woman, or even fight as much as he might have if a different man had been responsible for his apprehension. The Bishop's kindly face was stony as he helped

Mark steer John towards the barn, away from the game. As the two men guided John into the empty space, closing the door behind them, Mark could tell by the sounds of behind them that things were slowly getting back to normal; he hoped that someone was comforting and soothing Salome's fear.

"John, you must calm yourself," Bishop Fisher said, releasing the man's arm. Mark released John more slowly, able to feel the tension in the other man's body, aware of the potential for John to become more violent.

"Bishop—" John began, his voice harsh and grating. Mark stood back slightly, knowing that as John's equal, he could not speak at this moment; it was for the Bishop to speak to John, from his position of authority.

"I would like to know, John, why you felt the need to discipline a young woman who is not your daughter." Mark nodded slightly; it was a very good question. John sputtered.

"She is developing wayward ways, Bishop. I am courting her mother, and Salome does not have a father to discipline her. Sarah—Sarah will not do what is needed to protect her daughter from becoming immodest." The Bishop held up his hand.

"She is not your daughter, John King. As a fourteen-year-old girl, she is not a member of the church; even as a minister in this community, you do not have the right to restrict her freedoms."

"Bishop—Sarah Lapp has no man, no husband to keep her daughter in line!" Mark felt a wave of revulsion wash through him, but kept his expression carefully neutral. Words filled his heart, words of defense for Sarah, words of protection for Salome. But it was not his place to speak them now; it was not for him to defend Sarah Lapp. The bishop knew all of the members of the congregation well—if Bishop Fisher did not know that Sarah Lapp was a capable and devoted mother, then the older man was failing in his post.

"As you say, she has no husband; you are not married to her yet, and are in no position to act as a father to Salome. Even were you her mother's husband, I would have grave concerns over the way in which you choose to discipline." John's expression began to shift, and Mark saw that the Bishop's comments were beginning to filter through the other man's enraged mind.

"Salome needs someone to watch over her," John said, his voice taking on a grumbling, almost sulky-child tone.

"She has her Mamm to watch over her," the Bishop said firmly. "It is for Sarah to decide what discipline the girl needs, unless it is that you've already married Sarah?" The bishop raised one bushy, gray-blond eyebrow.

"Nee," John admitted. Mark could see that the man was still incensed, but John seemed to be at least controlling his anger in the presence of a higher authority. He sighed. "I understand what you are saying, Bishop. I will allow her to interact with the other youths her age." Mark bristled at the word 'allow'—knowing that in spite of John's contrite words, the man still viewed Salome—and by default, Sarah as well—as objects to control, rather than as people he cared about.

"Sarah Lapp is a perfectly capable Mamm," Mark said quickly, looking at the Bishop. "She guides and disciplines her daughter well." Bishop Fisher nodded, giving Mark a quick, almost sympathetic look.

"I would like to speak with John alone for a few moments, Mark," the bishop said. Mark bit back his frustrated words and nodded to the two men politely, taking a deep breath to clear his thoughts before he turned away to rejoin those watching the game.

CHAPTER NINETEEN

The moment that she heard John King shout her name angrily, Salome curled in on herself, cringing away from the others; she just knew that it would happen exactly the way it had before—that in an instant, she would feel the hard grip of John King's hand on her arm, that he would lead her away in shame and fear and pain away from the others. Only this time, she was sure, her mother would not be able to intervene. No one would intervene.

When she heard Bishop Fisher call John King's name, Salome looked up to see the bishop as well as the community's other minister, Mark Schrock, moving to intercept John, and a flood of relief washed through her. They were going to keep her safe; they were not going to let John hurt her. Salome felt tears stinging her eyes and struggled to regain her composure. The girls on both teams gathered around her, speaking softly, comforting her, and for a moment everything in the game stopped. Salome could see David Beiler, hovering a few feet away, watching with bright blue eyes full of worry for her fear. Salome took deep breaths. *The danger has passed. They took John away. The bishop is speaking with him now, along with Mark Schrock. I am safe.* She slowly felt the tremors beginning to ease as the fact of her safety filtered through Salome's panicked mind.

She said a silent prayer in her mind, turning her fear and her panic over to God. Salome had started to forget that there was a time in her life when she had barely known fear; in the time since John King had begun to court her mother, it seemed as though the shadow of apprehension had come to stay, hanging over her house and burdening her thoughts. But she had faith that God would find a way to keep her and her mother safe. She had to believe that there was some way for God to help her, to comfort her in her time of need.

"Are you alright, Salome?" her mother pushed through the press of her friends and Salome finished composing herself, taking a few quick, deep breaths and nodding to her Mamm.

"Just frightened, not hurt, Mamm," Salome said. She held Sarah Lapp's gaze for a long moment, wishing that she could tell her mother to simply never have anything more to do with John King. But she knew that there was no point in it; her Mamm was as frightened of John as Salome was, and if John wanted to continue courting, it would be difficult for Sarah Lapp to make herself gainsay him. Salome took a few more deep breaths and her Mamm, giving her a lingering, upset look, retreated back amongst the other adults of the community.

The buzzing hum of concerned conversation began to abate and Salome decided that she wanted nothing more than to get back into the game; she wanted to forget that anything had happened, and hope that after speaking with the bishop, John King would know that he needed to change his ways. "Let's get the game started again," Salome suggested, looking around at her friends with a kind of optimistic desperation in her eyes. They latched onto the idea, the other team taking up its position on the other side of the net.

"Let Salome serve," Martha Zook suggested, and Salome smiled weakly. Her serve was not wonderful, but she accepted the volleyball from one of her other friends, taking up her position. She spiked the ball, barely getting it over the net, but at least, Salome thought, the game was back in action, and she could once more forget about John King and his keen, critical gaze. She could go back to pretending that her life had never changed, that she was unafraid as ever. She could just be herself once more.

CHAPTER TWENTY

As Mark Schrock left the barn, Bishop Tom Fisher turned the fullness of his attention onto John King. He had long been concerned about John; he had hoped that as the man was brought more into the community by becoming a minister, that his impulse to control the lives of those around him would decrease. Although Tom had known John for a long time—had, indeed, been preparing to end his formal education when the man had been born—he had never been the kind of bishop to intervene in the lives of his community, even his ministers, directly unless there was cause.

The bishop had never had real troubles with any of the ministers chosen by the congregation; he kept himself carefully apart from the decision-making process, not wanting to interfere. It was for God to judge every man, and Tom knew that while he was responsible for helping to keep the peace within the community, he preferred for the rules to be observed in their strictest spirit: the people of the church would decide whether a man could be a minister, and if he had difficulties with one that could not be peaceably resolved, he would act only as the situation required, and never before.

Tom had been present at the straw frolic; he had seen the move that John King had made against Salome, had seen the fear on the girl's face. The bishop had also heard a great deal from multiple people within the community about the incident that had happened there. He had long known that John's particular trial in life was his lack of natural Gelassenheit, the inability to simply let things be as God would will. Many of the youth had been almost as frightened as Tom was certain Salome and Sarah had been at the incident—and some of the adults had been deeply concerned as well.

Abusive behavior was not unheard-of for Tom; he knew that while the ideals of the faith demanded avoidance of violence, cooperation, and peaceful resolution of conflict, there were some damaged souls, troubled people, within the community who grappled with their tempers and found it difficult to restrain themselves. He knew as well that much of John King's troubles stemmed from a difficult childhood, with a mother who was not as stable as one might wish. But while a child, undisciplined and immature, could be easily forgiven for temper tantrums and the venting of frustrations in destructive ways, for an adult member of the community, responsibility was the requirement. John King would have to be accountable for his lapses, and would have to do better. "John," Bishop

Fisher said, regarding the man steadily. "I saw the incident at the frolic a few weeks ago."

"Bishop—I am trying to do my best as a minister to bring Salome to a sense of her wrong..." Tom shook his head quickly.

"Nee, John, you will listen to me. Do not speak; you are still angry, and angry men will speak a thousand words they regret." The bishop, savvy in the ways of people after years serving as bishop of the congregation, and after fifty years of living in the midst of his community, waited for John to regain control over himself. He knew that lecturing an enraged man made little difference; if there was not the need to keep John King under some kind of control, Tom would have waited until the other man was calm to approach the subject. But the behavior that John had exhibited was absolute anathema. He was not even the husband of Sarah, not even the father of Salome; even if he had been, there would be deep concern throughout the community at the kind of controlling, abusive measures that he had already taken.

In his careful observations of Mrs. Lapp and her daughter, Tom had been only slightly less aware of the changes in their behavior than Mark Schrock had been. He had seen that Salome kept more to the home—a strange alteration, in light of the girl's social, sociable nature. The well-maintained comfort and ease, the resignation to the will of God and the untroubled way that the two Lapps approached the sometimes-difficult realities of life were an example to the whole community. But as the courtship between John and Sarah had continued, a doubtful, fearful cast had come over both Sarah's and Salome's faces, even when they were not around the man. That Salome avoided company, that she looked around her furtively whenever she was in a mixed group, told the bishop that John was taking measures in private that he was not quite daring enough to perform in public.

"I understand, Bishop," John King said begrudgingly. Tom took a deep breath, knowing that few of his words would be heeded; but they needed to be said.

"John, I've known you for most of your life; I was almost in my Rumspringa when you were born. Ever since that incident, I have been watching you and both of the Lapp women very closely." Tom paused to let his statement filter through John King's mind. It was true that Tom had been watching John closely; even when he had learned that John was courting Sarah Lapp, Tom had been somewhat concerned. The circumstances of John's first wife's passing had been just mysterious and abrupt enough to arouse some small suspicions, with what Tom Fisher knew about the other man. Tom continued, "I saw Salome's face when you shouted her name, John. She was frightened to the point that her face lost all color. That makes me think that you have attempted to control her, her mother or both of them before. In private. Am I right?"

Tom knew that he was; he needed for John to recognize for himself the errors he had made. The bishop did not want to try and force the revelation on his minister; but he had to make it clear to John that the behavior he had shown was disapproved of by the community as a whole.

"I do not require supervision to be a good husband or a good father," John said resentfully. The Bishop took a deep breath, giving himself patience.

"You require supervision because I am the bishop of this congregation, and you are a minister. I have an interest in making sure that you are fit for your position."

"I am a minister!" John's eyes fired with something that looked to Tom Fisher's gaze like pride, something like anger and hubris. The expression gave Tom some pain for John's sake, but he did not comment on it. "I want to make sure that Salome doesn't—" the bishop shook his head once more, patiently and calmly.

"John, it is not for you to make sure of anything. Remember your scripture. 'Take therefore no thought for the morrow: for the morrow shall take thought for the things of itself. Sufficient unto the day is the evil thereof.'" John's lips twitched and his nostrils flared in angry denial. "We are counseled by God, John, to trust in him. You are not trying to make sure; you are trying to control."

"But—Sarah will not discipline Salome the way that the girl needs." Tom raised his hands in a gesture of peace.

"It is as God wills, and it is to Sarah to discipline her daughter." Tom pinned John down with a sharp look. "I've long known of your need to control everything around you, John King. You seem to believe that if you can have absolute control, that nothing of misfortune will ever befall you—but in your need of control you become enraged at those things that are outside of your control." Tom paused again, letting John absorb what he was saying. "When those you try to control do not comply with your wishes, they suffer—and that is wrong."

The bishop knew that John would likely struggle with the burden of his need for control for the rest of his life; while Tom could offer the man comfort and counsel, and extend the words of the Bible, the important matter was to make sure that John would not lash out the way he already had shown himself capable of doing. A man's troubles did not excuse his actions.

Tom saw that John was struggling with himself, struggling with the rage that continued to simmer inside of him. He gave the man a moment, knowing that he must be patient and fair—not only to John as a minister, but to the man as a person. He spoke again, letting John feel the weight of the warning. "If you attempt to exert your control over Mrs. Lapp or her daughter in such a way as I saw you do weeks ago, then I will bring the community together to hear what you have done and listen to your defense. We will then decide whether you will remain a part of this community, or receive the Meidung."

THE END.

THANK YOU FOR READING!

And thank you for supporting us as independent authors. We hope you enjoyed reading this as much as we loved writing it! If so, we also hope you also enjoy the sample in the next chapter of Lancaster County Second Chances by Ruth Price.

You can find this book in ebook and paperback format at a variety of online booksellers.

Writing a review is the best thing you can do to keep indie authors like me and Sarah writing. (And if you find something in the book that – YIKES – makes you think it deserves less than 5-stars, drop me, Ruth, a line at ruth.price@globalgrafxpress.com and I'll fix it if I can.)

All the best,

Ruth Price & Sarah Carmichael

LANCASTER COUNTY SECOND CHANCES

When an Amish widow and widower, against all odds, begin to fall in love, will they have the faith to risk their hearts a second time?

After Katie Fisher's husband and young son are killed in a house fire, the young Amish widow returns to her parents' home broken-hearted with her faith in shambles. Katie can never imagine herself marrying again. But when 31-year-old Amish widower, Joseph Lapp, comes to Katie's district church service looking to hire an honest woman to help him take care of his three active, rambunctious children, Katie takes the plunge and accepts the position. Katie quickly finds herself falling in love with Joseph's children, and though Katie and Joseph cannot spend time together unsupervised due to the strict tenants of their Ordnung, the widow and widower find themselves growing closer in spirit as well. But when a new tragedy threatens the fragile future Katie and Joseph have begun to build, will the couple have the faith to risk a second chance at love?

CHAPTER ONE

Katie Olsen looked out the kitchen window. The sun was just coming up, and everyone but her *mamm* and younger sister were already out in the fields. It was spring, and the rising sun spread its beams over soft brown earth, ready for planting. The landscape was the same as she remembered. The gentle hills of her Lancaster County home seemed to be forever rolling away to the horizon. It had always been a comforting view.

She picked at the white cotton tablecloth with her fingers. It was the same familiar table cloth she had used as a child – the hand sewn border, the faint stain from the strawberry accident, the little uneven nubs that she had loved to rub with her fingers.

This plain white farmhouse still looked just the same as it had when she was six years old. The massive gray barn had seemed endless then, and it still looked huge. The freshly-tilled earth would soon be filled with movement and color and sound.

This farm had been her home. She had felt so comfortable in it, as if she herself had been a young plant springing up from her daed's fields. She had grown from this soil, like the oak trees overshadowing the house. Like her mamm's roses. Like the wheat that swayed and whispered secrets to the lavender twilight. Once, her world had been as safe and predictable as bud and bloom and harvest. It had seemed to her that nothing would ever change.

But everything had changed. She was 26 now. The familiar white farmhouse wasn't her home any longer. It was her parents' home.

The tablecloth, the house, the barn, the oak trees, and even the rolling hills, all of them belonged to the child she had been, not the young woman she had become.

For the past three months, she had been an increasingly uncomfortable guest in her parents' home.

Maybe even a burden.

Of course, her mamm and daed would never put it that way. And she did her best to help them around the house and with her little sister and brother.

But still.

Katie's fingertip raised the corner of a paper lying underneath her breakfast plate. Her mamm had "forgotten" it there this morning.

It was an Amish advertising circular. The headline read: Young Widowed Men Interested in Remarriage.

A cheerful voice interrupted Katie's thoughts.

"Why such a sad face, Katze?"

Katie pulled her lips into a smile and turned to face her 10-year-old sister, Bett.

"No sad face for you, Bett." She pulled her blonde giggle box of a sister into her arms and smiled. "Come, I will help you with your chores."

They walked out to the chicken coop and roused the hens. Katie had always liked gathering eggs – the sleepy, blinking hens, the feel of their soft feathers, the warm, smooth eggs.

Bett was skipping in her joy. "I'm glad you're back, Katze," she was saying, calling Katie by the nickname everyone in her family used. Bett's blue eyes were full of affection.

Katie stopped gathering eggs momentarily. She bit her lip. She wished she could say, I am glad to be back, but that would have been a lie, and she already had too many sins on her soul.

"I'm glad you are pleased," was what she said.

"Everyone is pleased," Bett nattered on. "Last Sunday I heard Mr. Hershberger say that you have a pleasing countenance and that you are a diligent worker. And Mr. Beiler said that he's glad you're back, and that it's a good thing."

Bett dug a toe into the dirt and smiled shyly up at Katie.

"I think they like you," she added, in a conspiratorial tone.

Katie stifled an impatient exclamation. Mr. Hershberger was 20 years her elder. He was bald and fat and had an ungovernable temper. And Mr. Beiler was 70 if he was a day and as shriveled as a stick. The last thing in the world she wanted was to attract the attention of men like Mr. Hershberger and Mr. Beiler.

Or, really, the attention of any man.

She closed her eyes and counted slowly to ten before saying, "I think that's all for now, Bett. Let's take these back."

Bett giggled and skipped along beside her. "I can't wait until I'm your age, Katze," she confided, "and all the men are asking after me."

Katie said nothing in reply, but she was wishing with all her soul that she could somehow revert to her sister's age and once again be a freckled, laughing child.

***

At dinner that night, the table was laden with baked bread and butter, beans and bacon, ham, baked potatoes, apple pie topped with cheese. It was good, solid farmhouse cooking, some of which Katie had made herself, but she had no appetite.

Katie's mamm shot her husband a glance. He straightened in his chair and cleared his throat.

"Are you feeling ill, Katze?" he rumbled.

"No, Daed," she replied.

"Eat, then."

She dutifully picked up a forkful of potatoes and put it into her mouth.

Katie retreated to bed immediately after dinner, pleading a throbbing head. Her parents had put her in her old bedroom. It still looked much the same as it had – the bare wooden floor, the plain single bed next to the big window overlooking the fields, the same starburst quilt that her grandmother had made for her when she born, with its red, blue, and green.

Even her old toys were still there – the old cotton doll and the stuffed bear that she had worn to shreds, all still lying at the bottom of the quilt chest at the foot of her bed.

There was the prayer book she had used as a child, still with her childish scrawls inside.

The old bedroom should have been a reassuring haven, but for Katie, it was oddly jarring – a reminder of what she wasn't anymore, and could never be again.

Just as she had always done, she knelt down beside the bed for her evening prayers. As a child, it had been easy and natural for her to pray to God. She had felt His presence everywhere.

But tonight, she found no words to say. Now, she didn't feel His presence at all.

She had not felt His presence for months. Sometimes, in her darkest moments, she even feared that God had…

The sound of a soft knock at Katie's bedroom door ended her devotions. Katie rose and opened the door to find her mamm standing outside. The candlelight touched her braided brown hair with gold.

"May I come in?"

"Of course." Katie sat down on the bed and patted the space beside her. Katie's mamm sat down quickly and put an arm around her. Her eyes looked worried.

"I shouldn't have left that advertisement on the table. I think I've upset you," she said softly. "I'm sorry. I didn't mean to."

"You have a right," Katie replied, looking down.

"It's not about our rights," her mamm corrected quickly. "Your daed and I, we just want to see you smile again. To come back again, just a little bit." She smoothed a tendril of Katie's soft brown hair back from her face. "It was too soon, maybe."

"You're not the only ones," Katie told her, with an unhappy grimace. "Bett told me today that Mr. Hershberger and Mr. Beiler were asking after me," Katie added, wrinkling her nose.

Her mamm burst out laughing and hugged her close. "Then I don't blame you for picking at your food tonight." She smiled. "It would trouble me, too."

Katie smiled in spite of herself, and her mamm laughed again. "There," she said tenderly, lifting Katie's chin. "That's what I was looking for. My Katze."

Suddenly everything that had happened, everything that she had lost, welled up in Katie's heart. "Oh, Mamm!" she cried, and sobbed as her mamm made soothing noises and rocked her back and forth like a child.

CHAPTER TWO

The next morning, Katie was up long before dawn and long before anyone else was awake. She dressed by the light of a single candle and went down to the empty kitchen. She put a piece of cheese between two slices of bread, wrapped it in a handkerchief, and put it in a bag.

She started a fire in the fireplace to make the house warm, put on her own coat, and went outside.

The predawn dark was still very damp and cold. A thick fog covered everything. Karl, her daed's old collie, was curled up in a box on the porch. He opened one eye and mustered a few thumps of his tail in greeting.

Katie bent down and ruffled his fur, then walked to the barn. Her old blue bicycle was still in the corner. She walked it out into the yard, adjusted the bag around the handlebars, and pushed off into the fog.

The beautiful pastures of Lancaster County slowly rolled past. At first, in the dark, she knew them by the sweet smell of freshly-turned earth, the faint sound of dogs barking far away, the lowing of a cow. Then the sky began to lighten, and the fog faded to reveal big, rolling hills, which, though dark brown now, would soon be alive with fresh green. Katie inhaled deeply. She loved the scent of freshly turned earth, of dew, of new things stirring in the grass.

She pedaled past the Iverson farm, the Johansen farm, the Muller farm. Each field conjured up faces and names from the past. Most of the boys had been blonde, gangly, and tall. A few had hinted that they might like to court with her. She almost smiled, remembering John Muller and his shy calf eyes.

Of course, they hadn't ended up together. She had left home five years ago and her parents told her that John hadn't shown interest in anyone else for a good two years. That is, until Laura Pedersen grew up and caught his eye.

A sudden pain in her shoulder made Katie grimace and slow her pace.

When she was Bett's age, Katie could have arrived in town within 30 minutes. But it was becoming clear that this time, it would take her twice that, if not longer. It wasn't the fog that hindered her – she knew every pebble in those well-worn roads. She could have ridden them with her eyes closed.

It was her shoulder. The damp made it ache, and she had to go slowly to avoid pulling it. Her bandages had only come off a week before, and she couldn't bear the thought of facing another doctor.

She closed her eyes and let the bicycle bounce freely down a long, straight slope. She tried to shut it out, but even this small reminder made her peaceful thoughts drift away like the morning mists.

It made the doctor's face come back again, as it had been coming back every day for the last three months.

"I'm sorry," he was saying, and put a hand on her arm. "Is there anything you'd like us to do?"

She heard herself screaming, *Gott im Himmel*!

She put a hand to her mouth, and momentarily the handlebars left her control. The bicycle bounced dangerously off a rock and she had to hit the brakes to keep the bicycle from crashing.

Gott...

The bicycle skidded to a stop, and Katie dug her heels into the gravel to keep herself from falling over. She could feel herself trembling. She tried again to pray, to plead, to feel something, but there was nothing.

Maybe she should never have left. Maybe God had meant her to stay here, to marry John Muller.

She must not have done God's will. Because surely, if she had done it, her life wouldn't have gone so horribly wrong.

God must be angry with her, so terribly…

Katie closed her eyes and stood very still, feeling the muffled pounding of her heart. Minutes passed. A door closed somewhere in the distance, a man's voice issued a short, sharp command, and a dog barked.

God did not strike her dead. The world did not end.

She put a hand to her eyes and pushed off again.

***

"*Guten morgen*, Katie!"

It wasn't hard for Katie to muster a smile for Elie Meissen. Elie's face was as plump and red as a ripe apple, and it was always smiling. Katie had never seen her in a bad mood, but if Elie had a fault, it was that she had the longest tongue in three counties. Elie loved to get news, and she loved even more to report it.

"Guten morgen, Elie Meissen."

The Meissens ran a store in town and made their living mainly off of the sale of quilts, furniture, and other handmade crafts to tourists.

Elie tilted her head to one side, like a bird. "What brings you to town, Katie?"

"I'm looking for a job," Katie replied. "I need work, and was wondering who might need help."

Elie's bright eyes sparkled with this new intelligence. "Ah! I wish we could help you, but we already have three women who make quilts." She put a finger to her lips. "Maybe I can ask around for you."

She waved Katie around to the back of the counter. "So you came on your bicycle? That's a fair way from your farm. Have you had your breakfast?"

Katie shrugged. "I have bread and cheese."

"Bah," Elie laughed. "Come back to the office and have pie and coffee."

Elie led the way to a small office with one wooden table and three chairs. There was a small counter on one wall, and it was covered with kitchen clutter. Elie pulled out a chair for Katie and poured a cup of steaming hot coffee. "Take a piece of pie. It's coconut cream from last night. So good." Elie put a plate on the table and licked her thumb.

Katie didn't feel especially hungry, but took a few bites to be polite. The pie was very good – rich and creamy and indulgent.

"I'm so glad you're back," Elie confided, pulling up a chair. "So much has happened since you left. Let me catch you up."

Katie stifled a sigh and braced herself. Elie was never happy until she had told all she knew. Or thought she knew.

"Terese Johansen spent *rumspringa* in Philadelphia running wild with the English, they say. She has decided to leave altogether and become a Presbyterian. Her parents are prostrated, I can tell you."

Katie was tempted to offer a tentative rebuke for Elie's gossip, but thought better of it. She was grateful that Elie was sharing news rather than asking painful questions.

Katie's annoyance softened. She was also sure that Elie's unusual forbearance was not accidental. Given Elie's love of gossip, her restraint on that point was an act of grace. Katie sipped her coffee and said nothing.

"And did you know that Martin Hoffer is the new bishop after old David Zurich died? Remember how we almost used to go to sleep during services?" She giggled. "Well, not anymore! No one can have any peace during his sermons, let alone sleep! He's the strictest bishop anyone can remember. So stern!" Her cheerful face grew scrunched up momentarily as she took a sip of coffee. "It gives me heartburn."

Katie's conscience stirred again, and again she squelched it.

"Oh!" Elie fanned her face. "And there's another newcomer besides you! Of course, you're not new, and he is, but you know what I mean. It's a widower with four *kinner*, a man named Joseph Lapp. He's from the next county. Quite good looking, so I hear. Tall. A little peaked, though."

Katie stirred uncomfortably, and Elie nattered on. "Of course, every woman in the county who has a grown daughter has set her cap for him. Though he's a little old for a girl."

A sudden ringing from the shop announced the arrival of a customer. Katie breathed a sigh of relief as Elie jumped up and finally tended to her own business.

Or almost tended to it. She could just hear the sound of a woman's voice and Elie's voice in reply. After the initial greetings, their voices lowered, but not before Katie heard the words, "Oh, the poor thing."

She sighed, shook out her skirt, and rose to leave.

CHAPTER THREE

That evening after dinner Katie went to bed early again. She undressed by the light of a candle, peeling off the plain blue dress and black stockings. She stood in front of the mirror. The sad young woman who looked back at her had soft, wavy brown hair, large, earnest green eyes, and a body that her mamm had once told her was "womanly."

Except for the stain. And now, the scar.

It was vain, and wrong, but she couldn't resist running her finger over the scar on her shoulder. Her skin was still tender from the surgery. The angry red color had faded, and the doctor had promised that it would continue to fade until it could hardly be seen. But at three months out, a faint splotch was still there, still visible, though barely, in the dim light.

The stain had been the size of a dinner plate. Its outline had been ragged and ugly. It had looked as if her right shoulder had been splashed with red wine. The purple birthmark had been her secret shame, and also her secret vanity. It had covered three inches of her upper arm, the right side of her neck, and two inches of her back.

She had hated it all her life, but her parents had told her that God loved her, and that they loved her, and that it made no difference – that it was vain to be concerned about things that did not endanger her health.

But in her vanity, she had chosen to have the hated mark removed anyway.

Katie knelt by the bed and clasped her hands. She tried to pray the prayers she had learned as a child, to be pious and meek, but something in her convulsed, and her grief suddenly came spilling out.

Oh, God, was it this? Was this why? So much, only for this?

Why not me, then?

The only reply was the sound of the candle sizzling as it wept its small tears. Katie searched her heart for any answer, any sense of God's nearness, any comfort.

Oh, God, where are you?

There was no sound, no spark of feeling. Nothing.

Sobs welled up in her throat, and her head drooped over the bed. She stopped trying to pray. It was useless. And she was too tired to spend another night with her hands over her face. She rose, blew out the candle, and slipped under the covers.

Katie was exhausted, and sleep came quickly. She felt as if her body was falling into some measureless depth, down into some infinity of sleep. Waves of unconsciousness closed over her, pushing her further and further down.

"Katze."

She turned her head and murmured softly...

THANK YOU FOR READING!

And thank you for supporting me as an independent author. I hope you enjoyed reading this as much as I loved writing it!

If so, you can find this book in eBook and paperback format at your favorite online booksellers.

Lastly, if you enjoyed this book and want to continue to support my writing, please leave me a review to let everyone know what you thought of my work. It's the best thing you can do to keep indie authors like me writing. (And if you find something in the book that – YIKES – makes you think it deserves less than 5-stars, drop me a line at ruth.price@globalgrafxpress.com and I'll fix it if I can.)

All the best,

RUTH PRICE

ABOUT THE AUTHORS

Ruth Price is a Pennsylvania native and devoted mother of four. After her youngest set off for college, she decided it was time to pursue her childhood dream to become a fiction writer. Drawing inspiration from her faith, her husband and love of her life Harold, and deep interest in Amish culture that stemmed from a childhood summer spent with her family on a Lancaster farm, Ruth began to pen the stories that had always jabbered away in her mind. Ruth believes that art at its best channels a higher good, and while she doesn't always reach that ideal, she hopes that her readers are entertained and inspired by her stories.

Sarah Carmichael has always loved telling stories, and when she met Ruth at a local farmer's market and the subject of writing came up, a friendship was born. Ruth and Sarah brainstormed intensively on Ruth's Yule Goat Calamity series, and worked together on The Long Run series and others. Through this collaboration, Sarah has also gained the confidence to start working on books on her own, which she will be publishing in the future. In her writing, Sarah strives to tell an entertaining story that shows the beauty of God through the seemingly small moments of our everyday lives.

www.ingramcontent.com/pod-product-compliance
Lightning Source LLC
Chambersburg PA
CBHW071237130626
46556CB00003B/1045